Contents

		page
Introduction		iv

PART ONE

| Chapter 1 | El Serrano Motel | 1 |
| Chapter 2 | Bloody Christmas | 2 |

PART TWO

Chapter 3	The Nite Owl Murders	14
Chapter 4	The Nite Owl Investigation	23
Chapter 5	Vincennes' Connections	35
Chapter 6	Quick Justice	40

PART THREE

| Chapter 7 | New Jobs | 42 |
| Chapter 8 | Bud White's Case | 49 |

PART FOUR

Chapter 9	Return to the Nite Owl	52
Chapter 10	Painful Truths	59
Chapter 11	The Pierce Patchett Connection	64

PART FIVE

Chapter 12	The Real Criminal?	73
Chapter 13	All in the Family	82
Chapter 14	The Nite Owl: Case Closed	92
Chapter 15	Absolute Justice?	97

| Activities | | 105 |

Introduction

Ed raised his glass and repeated what his father had taught him: "To the solving of crimes that demand absolute justice."

Christmas 1951 Los Angeles, a city where it is difficult to tell the difference between the good guys and the bad guys. At the Central Police Station, cops beat up six suspects who are being held in jail cells, and the event affects the careers of three detectives at the Los Angeles Police Department. Ed Exley begins his rise up through the LAPD. Bud White identifies his enemy. Jack Vincennes loses his role as "Mr. Hollywood."

April 14, 1953 Six people are murdered in one of the worst crimes the city has ever seen. Three suspects are in jail, but it will take five long years before the case is closed. For their own reasons, the three detectives search for absolute justice. But do they share the guilt?

James Ellroy has created an amazing world – real, criminal, and evil. This is crime writing at its best.

Ellroy was born in Los Angeles in 1948 and he was ten years old when his own mother was murdered. Since then, he has been interested in the criminal mind and the role of the police in a violent world.

His previous novels, *The Big Nowhere*, *The Black Dahlia*, *White Jazz* and *American Tabloid*, have won many prizes. Several of his books have been made into Hollywood movies, including *L.A. Confidential*. Actress Kim Basinger won an Oscar (Best Supporting Actress) for her role as Lynn Bracken in the movie.

James Ellroy now lives in Kansas with his wife.

PART ONE

Chapter 1 El Serrano Motel

February 21, 1950 Buzz Meeks left his car in the woods and struggled with his suitcase through the trees towards the El Serrano Motel, in Southern California. He was carrying $94,000 in cash, 18 pounds of pure heroin, two automatic weapons, a shotgun, and a knife. He needed to protect himself; he was not an innocent man. His crimes? He'd killed a Los Angeles policeman and had stolen the heroin and cash from Mickey Cohen's boys – some very dangerous gangsters. Now he was running from both the police and the gangsters, hoping to get out of the country before anyone figured out where he was.

He got to the motel and waited in one of the dark, dirty rooms. The plan was that Doc Englekling would send someone to get Buzz and take him to Guatemala – then Doc and his sons would hide the heroin and sell it later when things got quieter. If he could trust Doc and his boys, they'd all be rich. If he couldn't ... who knows. But right now he couldn't choose his friends.

Buzz laid out his weapons and thought of everything that could go wrong. The sun went down, but Buzz couldn't relax. Then two men – one fat, one thin – walked across the motel parking lot, smiling, looking friendly. The fat man said to Buzz, "We've got the airplane waiting. You ready to go?" Buzz smiled, then he recognized the thin man. It was Mal Lunceford, an ex-policeman, one of the criminal types. Buzz swung his shotgun around and covered them with bullets. The fat one died, but the thin one was safe behind him.

Buzz ran into his room, just in time to shoot the heads off two other men at the back window. Glass, blood, bits of brain flew

1

everywhere. Buzz could see three pairs of legs moving along the back wall behind the motel. He fired and got all six legs – then killed the three gunmen as they attempted to escape.

Buzz could taste blood, but shouted, "We got Meeks. He's dead!" He heard cheers and then three more men moved toward the motel room. He picked up an automatic and killed all of them. More shots from outside – how many more of them were there? Buzz was hit twice – once in the shoulder and once in the leg – and then he put two guns under his chest, lay on the floor and pretended to be dead. Silence. Then more footsteps and four men walked in holding shotguns. They spoke in whispers: "Dead meat." "Let's be real careful." Someone kicked Buzz. "Crazy fool." Buzz seized the foot and threw the man backwards. He spun around and shot all four of them. They didn't have time to raise their guns. Then behind him a voice said, "Hello, lad."

Buzz turned and faced Dudley Smith, a lieutenant from the Los Angeles Police Department. "Any last words, my lad?" Buzz raised his gun; Smith shot first. Meeks died as Lieutenant Smith stepped over him with the heavy suitcase in his hand.

Chapter 2 Bloody Christmas

December 24, 1951 Bud White sat outside City Hall in his unmarked police car. He checked the cases of alcohol in the back seat. He'd been happily accepting "Christmas presents" all day from friendly storekeepers. The Christmas party at the police station would be a big success. He checked his watch: Johnny Stompanato was 20 minutes late. Finally the door on the passenger side opened and Stompanato slid in. "Happy Christmas, Officer White."

Bud looked at Stompanato. He was a big, handsome, young Italian. Women of all ages found him sexy, although he wasn't the brightest star on the Christmas tree. He used to work for Mickey

Cohen as a bodyguard, but now Cohen was in jail for 3–7 years. Cohen was never accused of theft or murder. Like a lot of big gangsters, he went to jail because of problems with the tax department. These days Stompanato was unemployed and didn't have enough money to pay his rent.

"OK, Stomp, tell me your information."

"What? No 'Happy Holidays'? Didn't your mother teach you to be polite?"

"Listen, Johnny, I don't want to be your boyfriend. I heard you need money."

"Sad, but true. With Mickey and his lawyer pal Davey Goldman in jail, and no one looking after the business, my wallet is empty."

"I thought Mickey would leave you a nice fat envelope. I heard he was left with a pile of cash when Buzz Meeks left town."

"You heard wrong, officer. Buzz was helped out of town permanently, but no one found the cash or the heroin. Mickey was not pleased."

"So, what can you do for some cash tonight?"

"Shoplifter in Ohrbach's Department Store – fat, blond, about forty. Wearing a nice brown jacket and gray pants. Plus, here's your Christmas present: he likes to knock his wife around. Just your type. You can use those famous muscles of yours. That'll cost you 30 dollars."

Bud paid Johnny for his information and raced across town to Ohrbach's. He found Ralphie Kinnard and watched him slide some jewelry into his pocket. Bud followed the shoplifter to his house and saw him start an argument with his wife. Ralphie hit Mrs. Kinnard several times before Bud broke the door down and punched Ralphie until he begged Bud to stop.

Bud's goal in life was to punish all wife-beaters. If you hit your wife and Bud found out, he'd make sure you got ten hits for every one you gave, and Bud could hit harder than any wife-beater in the state of California. If Bud could beat up wife-beaters, maybe

3

his horrible dreams would stop. He was sixteen years old when he warned his father: "You touch Mother again and I'll kill you." It wasn't long before his father got drunk on cheap alcohol one night, came home and beat his mother to death with an iron bar. He'd tied Bud up and made him witness the whole thing. Then he left and Bud had to watch his mother's body decay. He wasn't found for a week. His father was put in prison for life and Bud was left with his mother's screams and the smell of her decaying body. Justice for Ralphie Kinnard meant no bad dreams for Bud tonight.

Back in his car, Bud received a radio call: "Two policemen attacked outside a bar on Riverside. Find and bring in six suspects. We know who they are from their car license numbers."

"Are the policemen badly hurt?" asked Bud.

"Yeah, it looks bad. Go to 48 Elm Street. Bring in Paco Sanchez, age 21, male Mexican."

Bud's partner, Dick Stensland, was already at Elm Street when he arrived. "Bud, I'm glad you're here. One of the Mexicans who attacked Brown and Helenowski is inside."

"How bad are our men?"

"Brown maybe has brain damage, and Helenowski maybe lost an eye."

"Two big maybes."

"Do you want a photograph?"

"No, of course not. Let's get him."

Bud and Stensland crashed through the door and had little trouble with Sanchez. They delivered him to the police station and were still in time for the Christmas party.

◆

Cavalcade Magazine, December 1951

THE EXLEYS: FATHER AND SON SERVE LOS ANGELES

Preston Exley, 57, owner of Exley Builders, the most successful building firm in California, started his career as a policeman. He served the Los Angeles Police Department loyally for 14 years and solved one of the most terrible crimes of our times: the 1934 Atherton case. Loren Atherton was found guilty of the violent murder of six children, including child TV star Willie Wennerholm.

Preston Exley's son Edmund, 29, began working for the LAPD in 1943, but his police career was interrupted by World War II. Ed went off to the war as a young soldier with no fighting experience and came home a hero. Since then he has been back with the LAPD, using his brains and experience to keep L.A. a safe place for all of us.

Your first impression of the two Exleys is that they are not typical policemen. They don't look like cops. They are both tall, thin, and expensively dressed. They don't talk like cops, and maybe they don't think like cops. They both graduated from college and they have a serious, intelligent attitude toward everything they do. And it seems that they can do almost anything. "Setting limits is against my nature," says the elder Exley.

What will the excellent Exleys be doing this Christmas Eve, for example? They will be celebrating Exley Builders' newest contract: the building of Dream-a-Dreamland. In the New Year, Preston Exley will build Raymond Dieterling's dream of a perfect amusement park for children of all ages. It will be a place where you can see your favorite Dieterling characters, such as Moochie Mouse and Danny Duck, and visit all of the imaginary places that you've seen in the Dieterling movies. The most amazing of all will be "Paul's World," named after Mr. Dieterling's teenage son who died tragically in a mountain accident in 1936. It will include an exciting ride down a snow-covered mountain which will remind everyone of the joy that filled Paul's short life.

Ed found his father chatting to a group of guests and asked to speak to him. "Dad, it's been another great Christmas party, but I'm on duty tonight. I'll have to go soon."

"Of course, Edmund, but first join me in my office. I'd like a word in private, and we haven't had our Christmas drink. The wine and the glasses are ready."

"After you, Dad."

"Edmund, we are an ambitious family. Tonight you've seen what I'll be working on in 1952. Son, what are your goals for the new year?"

"I want to be the youngest officer the Detective Department has ever had."

"Well, you've got the brains, but I worry about you. You're not one of the boys and you refuse to use muscle even when it's necessary."

"Father, I think there are other ways to solve crimes."

"Sometimes, but not always. You need to make friends with the right people and make sure you give them your support when they need it. You need to do whatever it takes to guarantee justice. Do you understand?"

"I do, Father. But, still, I'll find success in my own way. There are some things I won't do. And I don't need to be popular with everyone."

"OK, my young war hero, OK. Take a glass of wine."

Ed raised his glass and repeated what his father had taught him: "To the solving of crimes that demand absolute justice."

The phone rang. It was a call for Ed. Two police officers had been attacked earlier; the jail was full, and Ed was needed at the police station immediately. He left one party to find out what was going on at another one.

◆

Jack Vincennes was a cop, too, but he looked more like a movie star. He felt comfortable with the Hollywood crowd and lived their kind of life. Besides his police duties, he was the technical advisor to the popular TV police series, *Badge of Honor*. His job was to make sure that the actors knew how to walk and talk like real cops. He also had a very pleasant arrangement with Sid Hudgens, top writer for *Hush-Hush*, the magazine that had the inside information on all the stars. If Jack arrested any Hollywood stars, he made sure that *Hush-Hush* got the photographs and the story. And Sid Hudgens made sure that Jack got an envelope after each story appeared in *Hush-Hush*. It was a good deal for both men, but Jack wondered if he could really trust Hudgens. Sid had private files which contained secrets on everybody who was important or famous in Hollywood. Jack himself had secrets – who didn't? Did Sid Hudgens know about Jack's darkest secret?

In 1947, Jack had lost the balance in his life. He had begun to think he really was Mr. Hollywood instead of Officer Vincennes. First it was alcohol, and plenty of it, and then he moved up to drugs. He was still certain that he could do his job for the LAPD. Maybe the drugs gave him confidence.

On October 24 of that year, Jack was flying high on drugs and was sent out to arrest some heroin dealers at a dance club called the Malibu Rendezvous. He watched the scene and saw the heroin change hands, so he chased after the criminals. They started shooting at Jack, but neither his brain nor his muscles would do what he wanted them to do. He fired his gun again and again; two people were killed, but they weren't the heroin dealers. They were just an innocent old couple out for a breath of fresh air. The police doctors hid the truth; the newspapers reported that the criminals had shot the couple and that Jack was a hero. But Jack's memory was not so kind to him. He knew what he had done, but who else knew? Was the truth about the Malibu Rendezvous in Sid Hudgens' files? Jack gave up alcohol and drugs on October 25. He was a healthier but a much sadder man.

Now, on the evening of December 24, 1951, Jack was at his typewriter. He was working on Dudley Smith's report on gangster activity in L.A. since Mickey Cohen was sent to prison. Jack lit a cigarette and read through the report. It was obvious why Dudley needed his help: spelling and grammar weren't his strengths. So Jack could earn some points by getting the report ready for the big bosses. First topic: Smith thought that Cohen's main men, John Stompanato, Abe Teitlebaum, and Lee Vachss, would become good, honest citizens without Cohen around to guide them into criminal activities. This didn't sound right to

Jack. Mickey's boys were bad at birth. Smith said the LAPD should watch out for *new* faces that might want to control Mickey's old business interests.

New topic: February 1950 – murder of Buzz Meeks. Jack had heard that Meeks took a load of money and heroin from Mickey Cohen's boys, but the boys, with the help of some LAPD cops, found Meeks and filled him full of bullets. No sign of the cash or heroin. Dudley Smith had a different story for the bosses: Meeks buried the money and heroin before he was killed. The hiding place and killers were unknown. Jack smiled. Smith probably knew that someone from the LAPD was involved. He wanted to make sure that no blame was directed at the department.

The phone rang. "Narcotics Department, Vincennes speaking."

"Big V, it's me. You hungry for some cash?" It was Sid Hudgens.

"What's happening, Sid? Got something good?"

"Two pretty, young star-types are celebrating Christmas early with a nice little bag of marijuana. You catch them and I'll be there with my camera. And a hundred dollars for you, pal."

"Where is 'there'?" asked Jack.

"Maravilla, number 2245. Meet me there in half an hour. Don't be late."

At the scene, Sid set up the cameras and Jack kicked the door down. He surprised Tammy Reynolds and Rock Rockwell, two young Hollywood actors. They were sitting in their underwear, staring at the Christmas tree. Jack took them outside and Sid got his *Hush-Hush* story with some entertaining photographs. Jack looked through Tammy's drawers and closets. He didn't find any more drugs, but he found an interesting business card: *Fleur-de-Lis. 24 Hours a Day. Whatever you desire.* What else were these young people doing in their free time?

"Hey, Big V, good work. Nice seeing you. Nice seeing so much of Tammy and Rock, too. Thanks for the story." Sid blew a kiss at Jack and walked back to his car.

Jack wondered again how much Sid knew about him. Then he went back to the police department for the Christmas party. He had a case of alcohol in his car to add to the holiday spirit.

◆

It was after midnight and the Christmas party at the Central Police Station was getting wild. Everyone, except for Ed Exley and Jack Vincennes, had been drinking. Some of the cops were already asleep, but most were talking about what had happened to Officers Helenowski and Brown. The six Mexican suspects were in police cells, waiting to see what kind of justice the LAPD planned for them. The drunken cops told the story again and again, and each time, Helenowski and Brown got worse injuries and the Mexicans became more and more like cop butchers.

The loudest and most drunken voice belonged to Dick Stensland, Bud White's partner. Suddenly, Stensland went crazy and began demanding police justice. "Let's deal with those cop beaters. Let's give them a Christmas present they'll never forget."

Stensland picked up the keys and rushed to Cell 4. A crowd of drunken cops followed him, shouting: "Make them bleed for Helenowski and Brown, Stens!"

Stensland opened the cell and started hitting the first Mexican he could get his hands on. Soon the cell was full of cops beating up Mexicans. Bud knew this could mean big trouble for Stens and he pushed into the cell to stop his partner. But one of the Mexicans recognized Bud. "Hey, Mr. White! You beat up my friend José because he punched his wife. What's wrong with you?"

Bud turned and picked up the Mexican by the neck. He banged his head on the ceiling and then kicked him out of the cell. The Mexican ran into Jack Vincennes and annoyed him by getting blood on his $100 suit. Jack ended his insults with one good punch to the Mexican's chin.

"Stop this. That's an order," shouted Ed Exley. Either no one

9

heard him or no one considered following orders from a rich college boy. Exley started pouring the alcohol down the sink in the storeroom; he had to find a way to stop this shameful behavior. But Bud was looking for ways to protect Stensland. He closed the door on Exley and locked him in. He didn't want him to witness anything else that Stensland might do.

For the rest of the night Ed was locked in the small room with no windows, no telephone. He shouted and banged on the door, but no one came. Everyone was too busy beating up the six Mexicans. Then Ed decided to fight back with his brains. He wrote down every rule that had been broken and every word that he had heard spoken or shouted. He included names and times. His report could end the careers of every cop out there, but especially those of Stensland and White.

6:14 a.m. Someone unlocked the storeroom. Ed walked out without saying a word. He went to the phone and called for ambulances. The scene outside the cells almost made him faint.

♦

January was a slow month for Bud White. He got some useful information from Johnny Stompanato, and he used his muscle against a few wife-beaters, but the serious gangsters seemed to be waiting and watching. No one had stepped into Mickey Cohen's shoes.

Halfway through January, the six Mexicans who had attacked Brown and Helenowski walked out of jail. Their guilt hadn't been proved. People started saying that there was going to be trouble for the cops who beat them up, and Bud started worrying: What should he do? Talk to Stens? Check their stories? Find a good lawyer?

February was worse. The newspapers screamed: *LAPD Breaks the Law, Bloody Christmas: Six Innocent Citizens Demand Justice*.

Stensland called, "Bud, this could be trouble."

Bud said, "No joke, partner. We're up to our necks in it."

Ed Exley knew that "Bloody Christmas" was trouble for some, but it was his big opportunity. He wanted to show the public that the LAPD would punish all law-breakers, even if they were cops. In the process, he could get rid of the police officers that he considered unprofessional, especially Stensland and White, and he could expect to move up to an important position in the Detective Department. Before he took action, he talked to his father.

"Edmund, you've made a very difficult choice. Are you sure that you're strong enough to go against other police officers? You know that every cop in L.A. will hate you for telling the truth. They'll make your life in the Detective Department pure hell."

"I know, Father, but I'm ready. The police are not above the law."

Ed returned to his apartment and studied the case that had made his father a hero. The six children in the Atherton case were not only murdered, but also cut into pieces. At first there were no clues, but Preston Exley discovered a madman who had been arrested for stealing blood from a blood bank and drinking it. He searched the madman's apartment and found hell. Parts of bodies, bottles of blood, a "perfect" child on a bed of ice. The killer had sewed parts of different bodies together to make it. The face had come from the eight-year-old actor, Wee Willie Wennerholm, one of Ray Dieterling's stars. The suspect, Loren Atherton, was judged guilty and hanged. Preston Exley had photographed the bodies in Atherton's apartment, but very few people had ever seen the pictures. Ed looked at them again now. Hell.

Ed relived his own hell that night, too. He was the only person on earth who knew that he was a coward, not a war hero. He had not been a brilliant soldier, and he was afraid to come home after the war to Preston Exley and the LAPD without doing something brave and heroic. Finally, he was alone; all of the other men in his group had been killed. He came across a pile of dead Japanese soldiers and worked out a plan. He arranged the bodies, filled them full of bullets and set fire to them. He claimed that he had killed them all and his story was believed. He returned home a hero. Ed lived with his past; his father doubted his strength as a cop, but Ed knew that he could do anything to get what he wanted. He also understood that most men have dark secrets.

Ed Exley went to William Parker, captain of the LAPD, and gave him the full report of Bloody Christmas. Parker allowed Ed to investigate the whole affair. Every officer who had been at the Central Police Station on December 25, 1951 was brought in and questioned by Dudley Smith. Ed watched the interviews from behind a two-way mirror. The cops couldn't see him, but it wasn't long before everyone at the LAPD knew that Ed was willing to put a knife in police officers' backs.

Bud White's interview was very short. "Officer White, you have a chance to cooperate. Will you tell us what happened that night at the Central Station?" asked Dudley Smith.

"No, sir, I will not. I will not speak against other police officers," said Bud in a calm voice.

"Lad, we know you had reasons for doing what you did. You were heard saying, 'This is disgusting.' You tried to stop Dick Stensland. Tell us what happened and you'll be OK."

"No, sir. I will not speak against other police officers."

"Lad, you will lose your position in this department. You must speak now."

"No, sir."

"Get out of here, White." Dudley Smith said, but he smiled to himself very slightly. Bud stared at the hidden face on the other side of the mirror with pure hatred.

Dick Stensland also refused to talk about Bloody Christmas. Jack Vincennes made a deal with Parker and Smith; he kept his job by speaking against several officers who were ready to retire. Exley made sure that White lost his job and that Stensland was sent to prison. Vincennes was moved out of the Narcotics Department.

Preston Exley was right: Ed moved up to the Detective Department, but no one would speak to him. The whole LAPD hated him for his role in Bloody Christmas.

◆

Bud White sat in a bar, feeling deeply depressed. No gun, no job, no purpose. He was unenthusiastically trying to start a conversation with the woman sitting beside him when he heard a familiar voice. "Hello, lad. Can I have a word?" asked Dudley Smith.

"Is this business, Lieutenant?" asked Bud.

"Definitely. Say good night to your new friend and come over to my table. Sit with an old and true friend," said Smith.

"OK, what's going on? You know I've lost my job," said Bud as he sat down.

"Relax, lad. I admire your work and your attitude to the criminals in this town. I admire the way you get justice. I want you to work directly for me."

"For you? Doing what?" asked Bud.

"I want you to return to duty as a police officer and help me contain crime. We'll keep it outside the limits of our fair city," explained Smith.

"Lieutenant, is this really a deal? Can you really do this?"

"You are too valuable to lose, lad. You can come back to work tomorrow morning."

"Why are you doing this for me?" asked Bud.

"It's a muscle job and a shooting job. It's a job where you don't ask a lot of questions. It's my containment plan. Do you understand?" asked Smith.

"I understand, Lieutenant. But what will Exley say?" asked Bud.

"Do we care?"

"Not at all. Just keep him away from me," said Bud with a smile on his face.

PART TWO

Chapter 3 The Nite Owl Murders

April 14, 1953 Detective Sergeant Ed Exley looked around and smiled at the well-organized, empty office. No one else enjoyed filling in official forms and writing police reports.like Ed did. All of the information that came across his desk helped him understand the criminal brain. He noticed every detail. Anyway, he had no choice. At the moment he wasn't trusted with real detective work, so he concentrated on paperwork:

4/9/53	female shoplifter: complaints from four stores
4/10/53	waiter kicked to death; told customers to stop smoking
4/11/53	several reports over two-week period: 3–4 young black men firing shotguns in Griffith Park, driving purple car – probably a Mercury, 1950 model

Ed finished the weekly crime report and walked to the parking lot. Two men dressed as Danny Duck and Moochie Mouse were waiting for him. They knocked him down, kicked him in the stomach and face, and then took a photograph of him as he lay bleeding on the ground. As the two men ran away, Ed recognized the voices and laughs of Dick Stensland and Bud White – his enemies since Bloody Christmas. Ed coughed blood and swore that he would get revenge.

◆

Over in the Vice Department, Detective Sergeant Jack Vincennes was bored. He wanted to return to Narcotics, but he couldn't move until he solved at least one important case. Maybe his boss, Russ Millard, had the case he needed today.

"Gentlemen," Millard said to his detectives. "Something new and different: high-class pornography. No one knows where it's being produced and we don't have pictures of the models in our files. Your job? Find out who's making the stuff and who's selling it."

Jack felt the beginning of a headache. He had no interest in pornography. Millard handed him one of the magazines and he looked through it and yawned. Then he saw a photo of Bobby Inge, a 30-year-old male prostitute that he had arrested for possessing marijuana about a year ago.

Millard said, "Do you see any familiar faces, Vincennes?"

"No, sir," Jack replied, keeping the information on Inge to himself. "Where did you find this stuff, captain?"

"In a garbage can on Charleville Street. Why?"

"I know that part of town. Is it OK if I go over there and talk to a few people?"

"Fine, Vincennes. If you solve this one you'll be one step closer to your old fun and games in Narcotics," said Millard.

Jack left the police department with the feeling that this case was already solved. He was sure that Bobby Inge would lead him to the big boys who were making real money from the pornography. Blue skies, a big yellow sun in the sky. Jack headed toward 9849 Charleville to talk to Mrs. Loretta Downey, owner of the building where the magazines had been found.

Jack held up the magazines. "Ma'am, where did you find this material?"

"In the garbage cans – right at the top. Those pictures are disgusting. You should put those people in jail for a hundred years. It's against the laws of nature!"

"Well, Mrs. Downey, maybe you can help me put them away. Do you recognize this man?" Jack showed the old woman a recent photograph of Bobby Inge with his clothes on.

"Yes, I've seen him lots of times. He visits the mother and son in Apartment 3."

"Are they at home now?" asked Jack.

"No, I saw them both leave early this morning. Will you give me a reward for helping you?" demanded the old woman.

"Sure, I'll send you a personal check. Thanks for your help." Jack could see someone watching him from behind the curtains in Apartment 3. He walked calmly back to his car and then raced across town to Bobby Inge's neat little house.

By the time Jack got there, Inge's place had been cleaned out. The closets and drawers were empty. Someone from Mrs. Downey's building had probably warned Inge. Jack looked around the house but couldn't find any clues. Then he looked out the window and noticed that there was a garbage can on the sidewalk in front of each house. It must be garbage day!

Jack ran out and opened the can in front of Inge's house. He found the prize he'd been hoping for: three more copies of the porn magazine. Clearly Inge had not wanted to risk getting caught with them in his car and had thrown them out. Jack turned the pages quickly. It was the same stuff until the end. These magazines had an extra ten pages with something special: naked bodies, cut into pieces, with blood pouring from the cut-off arms, legs and heads. The pictures were horrible and somehow beautiful at the same time. An artist had, Jack guessed, created these false scenes by cutting up photos and adding artificial blood. The models weren't really dead and hadn't actually been cut into pieces. The whole idea was sick, but Jack couldn't stop looking at the pictures. When he reached the last page a business card fell out: *Fleur-de-Lis, Whatever You Desire*.

Jack had seen that card before. He saw a pay phone and called Sid Hudgens.

"*Hush-Hush*, give me some dirt," answered Sid.

"Sid, it's Vincennes."

"Big V. Where have you been? I need some good stories," said Sid in his friendly voice.

"Sid, I'm chasing some pornographic magazines. Shiny black covers. Very expensive literature. New faces. Clever stuff. Have you heard anything about it?" Jack asked.

"No, nothing at all," Sid said quickly. Just a little too quickly.

16

"What about a male prostitute named Bobby Inge? Or a place called Fleur-de-Lis?"

"Never heard of him or your magazines or this Fleur-de-whatever. It sounds like secret stuff, and the thing about secrets, Jackie, is that everybody's got them. Call me when you have a story." Sid's voice sounded nasty – a different Sid, not the one Jack knew. And why was he talking about secrets? Was it a warning? Did Sid know all about the Malibu Rendezvous in 1947?

◆

Ed Exley found an envelope on his desk on the morning of April 14. Inside was a photograph of himself, bleeding and frightened. No message, but he knew what it meant. It was White and Stensland's insurance. If Ed made things difficult for them, the whole world would see the photo of a weak, defeated Exley.

Now it was 6 a.m. and Ed was alone in the Detective Department. An emergency call came through: "Calling all departments. Nite Owl Café, 1824 Cherokee Street! Theft and murder! At least four dead! Go to the scene immediately!"

No one else around. This could be Ed's own case. He got to Cherokee Street like lightning. A policeman in uniform hurried over to him, "It looks like there are several dead. The bodies are all in the big refrigerator in the back, swimming in blood."

Ed pushed open the door, which had a sign on it: "Closed due to illness." He saw an empty cash drawer, broken plates, food on the floor and then the enormous refrigerator. Brains, blood, and bullets marked the walls. The bodies lay in two feet of blood. It was impossible to know how many there were – maybe five or six. Dozens of shotgun bullets floated in the blood.

Ed remembered: *several reports over two-week period: 3–4 young black men, firing shotguns in Griffith Park, driving a purple car – probably a Mercury, 1950 model*. Ed called to the young policeman, "Start asking questions. Did anyone see any cars parked outside this morning? Find out what kind of cars and what color."

Ed pushed open the door of the Nite Owl and saw newspaper reporters. Before he could talk to them, he heard a familiar voice, "Go home, lad. I'm in charge here now."

♦

The main hall at the LAPD was filled from floor to ceiling with detectives. Lieutenant Dudley Smith took the microphone, "Lads, you know why we're here: the Nite Owl murders. It's one of the nastiest crimes this city has ever seen. The citizens of Los Angeles demand immediate justice. We have some solid clues and we will give the people what they demand."

"What do we know, lieutenant?" asked a detective from the back of the room.

"Six dead. Three men and three women. One man and two women were employees of the café. The three others were customers. The cash drawer, purses and wallets were empty. It seems that six people were killed for a few dollars."

"How many gunmen, sir?" asked another voice.

"Our reports say there were three. They left 45 shotgun bullets in the bodies and in the walls of the refrigerator. Something went wrong with the robbery, or the killers were just crazy animals."

"What are our solid clues, lieutenant?" shouted someone else.

Captain Parker took the microphone. "We've had four crime reports over the past two weeks about three black youths firing shotguns in Griffith Park late at night. Witnesses say they were driving a 1950 purple Mercury. Policemen at the Nite Owl crime scene interviewed a van driver who saw a purple Mercury, 1950 model, parked across from the Nite Owl at about 3 a.m. this morning. Lieutenant Smith will give you the names of people who own a 1950 purple Mercury. Gentlemen, go out and find the killers. Use all necessary force."

Bud White smiled. The real message: *find the murderers and kill them.*

Jack Vincennes and Sergeant Cal Denton had three names and

18

addresses to check. The first purple Mercury they found had no tires and had grass and flowers growing through the engine. They had more luck with the second car. Denton knocked on the door of Leonard Bidwell's house.

"Mr. Bidwell. We've got a couple of questions for you," said Denton as the door opened.

"I'm an honest citizen, officer," said Bidwell.

"Where were you and your car last night at 3 a.m.?" asked Vincennes.

"I was in bed and the car was right there, where you see it now."

"Any proof?" demanded Denton.

"Yeah, sure. I've got a wife and six children inside. I don't go anywhere at 3 a.m. Why are you interested in my car?" asked Bidwell.

"Someone with a purple Mercury was doing bad things last night. Do you know anyone else with a car like yours?" inquired Vincennes.

"Sure. We've got a club, the Purple Pagans."

"Why don't you look at our list and tell us if you recognize any bad characters. Just point, you don't even have to name names."

"Oh, man," said Bidwell, looking at the list, "I don't want any trouble, but that one, he's real trouble. He's crazy. Loves to party with a shotgun and enjoys shooting dogs. We wouldn't let him join the Purple Pagans. He's too wild – him and his boys, Leroy and Tyrone."

"Sugar Ray Coates. Thanks, Leonard," shouted Vincennes as he and Denton raced to their cars. They planned to get to Coates before anyone else did.

The Tevere Hotel: a cheap hotel above a Chinese laundry. They found Coates' room and kicked down the door. The young black man inside put up his hands immediately, but Denton aimed his gun at his head anyway. Jack stopped him shooting at Coates' head, but the young man tried to run out the door. Jack knocked him down with two quick punches to the head.

"Where are your friends, Sugar Ray? Where are Leroy and Tyrone?" shouted Jack.

"Next room," Coates managed to say through broken, bloody teeth.

Vincennes kicked another door down but didn't wake up Leroy Fontaine and Tyrone Jones. They were either drunk or on drugs. Before the policemen took the suspects away, they found two boxes of 50 shotgun bullets on the chest of drawers. One box was almost empty.

Captain Parker read Jack Vincennes' report. Three black male youths in jail, waiting to be questioned. One of them, Sugar Ray Coates, owned a 1950 purple Mercury, but it had not been found. Shotgun bullets had been found in Fontaine and Jones's room, but no shotguns or other weapons. No large amounts of cash or coins. No clothes with blood on them, but Sugar Ray had been seen burning some clothes behind his building at 7 a.m. All three suspects had covered their hands with medicinal alcohol which made it impossible to test for gun powder. They had all spent time in jail when they were teenagers.

Parker called in Ed Exley. "Ed, we need to find the car and the shotguns, but I also want confessions. We need to solve this case quickly. If you can persuade them to talk, you'll have my job one day. Can you do it?"

Ed said, "Yes, sir."

The three suspects were each in a different room. Parker and other police officers could hear and see everything that happened in these rooms. Ed talked to Sugar Ray Coates first. After some easy questions, Ed said, "You know you could be in prison for life for this."

"This *what*, man?" asked Sugar Ray.

"This very nasty crime. What did you do with your car?" asked Ed.

"It's safe."

"What about your shotguns?"

"Don't know about no shotguns," said Ray.

"Where were you at 3 o'clock this morning?" asked Ed.

"In my bed asleep. Where do you think?"

"Did you take some drugs to help you sleep? Did Leroy and Tyrone give you something?"

"Those two? They take drugs – not me. They're stupid, like dogs. They got cheap stuff from that crazy Roland Navarette."

"I heard you like to shoot dogs, Ray. Is that true?"

"Dogs don't have no reason to live," said Ray.

"Like some people?" asked Ed.

"Yeah, like Tyrone and Leroy."

"But you're smart. You give me something on Tyrone and Leroy and you can make things easier for yourself. You'll go to jail for a few years, find yourself a nice boyfriend ..."

"Hey, cop, I don't like boys. That's Tyrone, not me," said Ray. "I like women."

"So you must feel really bad about killing three innocent women this morning."

"I DIDN'T KILL NOBODY!" shouted Ray.

"You burned your clothes this morning and you can't find your car or your shotguns. Things don't look good for you, Ray. Six people are dead. You'll hang for that unless you can prove you were somewhere else. You think about it. I'll be back in a few minutes. You think hard."

Ed went into the next room to talk to Tyrone Jones, the youngest of the three suspects. He was already shaking and crying. Ed knew he needed to talk. "Well, Tyrone, your friend Ray says you took some drugs last night and got yourself into some bad trouble," commented Ed calmly.

"It wasn't my fault. It was all Ray's idea," said Tyrone.

"What idea was that?"

"About the woman," said Tyrone, starting to cry again.

"You mean the three women you killed?" asked Ed.

"WE DIDN'T KILL NOBODY!" cried Tyrone.

"Well, you're acting very guilty if you didn't do anything. What happened last night, Tyrone? Were you out looking for boys? Ray says you like boys. Is that right?" Ed whispered cruelly.

"No! I like girls. I kept telling Ray and finally he said that he'd find one for me and I could prove it," said Tyrone in a rush.

"And did he? Did Ray find you a girl?" asked Ed.

"Yeah, she was for all of us. But we didn't kill her. We just used her last night. She's not dead or anything. Why do you think we murdered her?"

"Tell us where she is. Where did you leave her?"

"I can't. Ray and Leroy'll kill me."

"Tell me, Tyrone," Ed demanded. "It's your only chance. If this girl can't tell us where you were last night, you'll be accused of murdering six people. Where is she?"

"No, I can't," cried Tyrone. "I can't tell."

At that moment, the door flew open. Bud White lifted Tyrone out of the chair, threw him against the wall and put a gun in his mouth. "You tell me now or you're dead meat," threatened Bud. He pushed the gun deeper into Tyrone's mouth. "Where's the girl?"

Tyrone was frozen with fear. "S-ss-sylvester F-fitch, 109 and Avalon Street, gray corner house, please don't hurt me," begged Tyrone.

Bud ran out. Tyrone fainted. Ed tried to stand up, but his legs wouldn't support him.

♦

Dudley Smith drove the first car, with Bud White beside him. When they got to Avalon Street, Bud said, "Boss, he's mine."

Dudley smiled, "No problem, lad."

Up the back stairs, through an open door. Bud walked into a dark house with loud music playing in one of the rooms. Through the first open door he could see a frightened young woman, naked and tied to a bed. He went on to the living room and saw

22

Sylvester Fitch, sitting at a table drinking coffee. He saw Bud. "No, sir. I don't want no trouble here."

Bud shot him in the face and poured coffee over him. He found Fitch's gun, fired it at the wall and put the gun in the dead man's hand; Bud wouldn't shoot a man who didn't have a weapon. Then he called for an ambulance.

Chapter 4 The Nite Owl Investigation

Captain Parker said, "Ed, you were brilliant the other day. You knew how to squeeze Sugar Ray and his pals and make them talk. I don't like Bud White's approach, but together you two got the results we wanted. Now we just have to persuade the Mexican girl to give us her story."

Ed picked up a report form: *Inez Soto, age 21. A college student.* "Has anyone spoken to her?" he asked.

"Bud White went to the hospital with her, but no one has spoken to her for 36 hours. What do you think, Ed? Did the three blacks do the Nite Owl?"

"I'm not sure, sir. It might be something completely different. The blacks acted guilty in the interview, but they were guilty of the wrong crime. They couldn't have done the Nite Owl murders and have been with Inez Soto at 3 a.m.," Ed explained.

"Get to the hospital, Ed. Make sure Miss Soto talks," ordered Parker.

Ed reached the hospital as Bud White was walking out. "Leave her alone, Exley. She doesn't need your badge and a police interview right now," said Bud.

"White, don't you want to solve this case? Or are you upset because there's no one else for you to beat up or kill?" asked Ed.

"In different circumstances, I'd eat you for that."

"I'll get you one day, White. Before you do anything else to me," threatened Ed.

Bud looked directly into Ed's eyes, "Oh, yeah? War hero, huh?

Did those Japanese soldiers roll over for you?"

The "war hero" looked down and walked away.

In Inez's hospital room, Ed said, "Miss Soto, I'm sorry we don't have a lot of time. Your information is very important right now. Please tell me what happened on the night that the three men kidnapped you."

"They aren't men! They're animals!" whispered Inez.

"I know, Miss Soto, but they're suspects in a murder case, too. We need to find out if they had time to commit both crimes," explained Ed.

"They had time. They tied me up and used me. Then they gave me to Sylvester Fitch. I want them dead. I heard the radio. They did both crimes."

"Miss Soto, you must tell me everything and tell me what time the things happened."

"I won't remember any more details. I refuse to think about that night. It's too painful."

"Miss Soto, I want to help you."

"You ruined my life. You said those animals might not be guilty because of me. Officer White is the hero. He saved me and he killed that other animal, Fitch. Why didn't you kill those other three?"

◆

Bud arrived at work early on April 19 and found a report on his desk from Dudley Smith:

Lad, I still think that the three black youths are our murderers, but we must do things the right way. Check the backgrounds and recent activities of these three Nite Owl victims.

1 *Susan Lefferts*, white female, 21 years old, no criminal record. Born in San Bernardino, California. Salesgirl at Bullocks Department Store.
2 *Delbert Cathcart*, also known as "Duke," white male, 39 years old. Jail time for selling prostitutes. No regular job.
3 *Mal Lunceford*, 41 years old. Former LAPD officer. Career ended after

11 years because of poor performance. Night guard at Furman's Box Factory. No known address.

Bud went into the main detective office. It was already busy. Every man in the department was working on the Nite Owl case from morning to night. Bud checked the information on Lunceford. He had been a lazy, dishonest cop. Recently he had been working at Furman's, sleeping in a tent behind the factory and keeping warm in the Nite Owl during his free time. It seemed he had been in the wrong place at the wrong time on April 14. Bud decided to check on Lunceford's 11 years as a policeman. He went to the "L" cabinet and got a surprise. There was nothing on Lunceford – maybe he was so lazy that he hadn't done enough work to make a file. Strange.

Bud moved on to "Duke" Cathcart. His paperwork led him to a list of nine prostitutes who had worked for Cathcart over the last five years. Two were dead from sexual diseases, three had left the state, no information on two others, and names and addresses for the remaining two: "Feather" Royko and "Sinful Cindy" Benavides. Bud sent a cop out to bring these last two in for questioning.

Duke's two prostitutes knew about the murders and were willing to come to the police station. They looked bad in the early morning sun. Too much make-up, too many late nights. Bud said, "So you read the papers?"

Feather Royko said, "Yeah. Poor Dukey."

"Was he important to you? Will you miss him?" asked Bud.

"Dukey was Dukey. He didn't pay us very much, but he never hit any of the girls who worked for him. There's just us now and his girlfriend. She's only about 15 years old. We're the only ones left," said Cindy.

"What happened? He had nine girls working for him at one time."

"He was a dreamer. He'd get a big idea and forget about his prostitutes. He had a new dream lately. He was really excited and nervous about it." Cindy had her lipstick out, putting a fresh layer of red on top of several old layers.

"What was this new idea about?" asked Bud.

"He was going to sell some sick pornography. He was sure that he'd make a fortune. He thought that lots of rich people would want it. He thought it was really high-class. A step up for old Dukey, but I don't know if the deal was working. Dukey's dreams didn't usually come true."

"What about the girlfriend? Where did she come from?" asked Bud.

"Dukey found her working as a prostitute about a year ago. He liked having a really young girlfriend so he paid her to stop working. She never had anything before. Dukey let her go out and buy clothes and magazines, then she'd watch TV all day and wait for Dukey to visit. She'd do anything for him. Maybe she could tell you about his new dream," said Feather.

"Name and address?"

"Kathy Janeway. You'll find her at the Sea View Motel in Buena Vista," said Cindy.

Bud had two addresses to check: Duke Cathcart's apartment and the Sea View Motel.

Cathcart had lived in a cheap, one-bedroom place on Vendome Street. Everything was clean and tidy, but Bud made a professional search and noticed one thing that was a bit out of order. Cathcart had a neat pile of telephone books. They all looked new except for the one for San Bernardino. This one was open to the pages for "print shops" and Cathcart had put a circle around one of the shops in the list.

Bud took the San Bernardino book with him and got back in his car. Susan Lefferts was from San Bernardino, but the reports said she didn't know Cathcart or Lunceford. They had all been sitting at separate tables at the Nite Owl. But the police report said Lefferts had been going to Cathcart's table when the shooting started. Strange.

Bud had heard that the Vice Department was working on a pornography case. Four detectives were chasing some pornographic magazines, but they hadn't reported any clues. Was there a connection? Was the Nite Owl just a robbery that had gone wrong? Bud could take this case away from Ed Exley. He could be a real detective and not just a muscle man, but he was also afraid. He was the only person with this information, and he couldn't tell anyone yet – not even Dudley Smith. And Dudley would not be happy if he found out that Bud was thinking for himself.

Next stop: the Sea View Motel. When he drove into the parking lot, there were already two police cars outside the motel office. The cops were talking to the manager. "Detective Bud White, LAPD. What's happening, officers?" asked Bud.

"A shooting in room 17. Young girl – maybe fifteen or sixteen – murdered. We've sent for an ambulance. We're getting details about the girl now," reported one of the policemen.

"I'll have a look at the room," said Bud.

He wanted to get to the room before any other detectives arrived. It looked like a teenager's bedroom. There were magazines, potato chips, cans of soft drinks, a pile of make-up and about fifteen furry toy animals. Bud searched quickly for anything connected with Duke Cathcart and found what he was looking for. Inside Kathy Janeway's make-up bag, Bud found a business card: *Fleur-de-Lis: Whatever You Desire*. On the back someone had written: *Call Mr. Patchett, Brentwood 68143*.

Bud returned to the police station and found a message on his desk: *Lad, We haven't talked lately. Meet me tonight at the Pacific Dining Car for dinner – 9:30. D.S.*

At the restaurant that evening, Dudley Smith had some uncomfortable questions for Bud. "Lad, I heard that you were at a murder scene this morning. Why didn't I get a report?"

"I was checking into Duke Cathcart's background and talked to his two prostitutes. They didn't have any information, but they gave me the name of his last girlfriend. When I got to her motel

27

she was dead. I didn't think that her murder could have anything to do with the Nite Owl so I didn't report it," explained Bud.

"Well, lad, you're probably right about that, but I need to know everything that is connected to the case, even if it doesn't seem important. Give me full, daily reports."

"Sure, Boss."

"Right. I hope the Nite Owl will be closed soon. I have Captain Parker's OK on my new containment plan and I want you to join me on that. You'll be my second in command."

"That sounds good, Boss."

Bud left the restaurant knowing that he'd lied to Lieutenant Smith and that he wasn't going to give him a report on his next visit either. He would have to be very careful.

Bud's next stop was Pierce Patchett's house. He hadn't had any trouble finding the address of such a successful, well-known businessman. He parked and walked up to the very fashionable house. Mr. Patchett himself answered the door.

"Are you Pierce Patchett?" asked Bud.

"I am. Are you a policeman?" asked Patchett.

"Yeah, Officer Bud White. I'm a detective. I'm trying to solve a murder."

"Oh, really? And how do you think that I can help you?"

"Did you know Duke Cathcart? He was murdered on April 14 at the Nite Owl Café."

"Yes, I did some business with him once. But that was more than five years ago."

"What kind of business?" asked Bud.

"Do you care about all criminal activities or just your murder case?"

"I'm not concerned about anything else today, just the murder case, so you can talk."

"Well, listen closely – you'll get this information only one time. I have prostitutes who work for me. They are special young ladies who remind my customers of Hollywood stars. About five years ago Cathcart had a new girl, Lynn Bracken. She was much too beautiful to be working for him – and she looked a lot like Veronica Lake. I bought her 'contract' from him, and she's been with me since then. I treat my girls very well; we have a good business relationship. I'll give you her address and you can talk to her about Cathcart," explained Patchett.

"Thanks, Mr. Patchett. By the way, did you get this house and the big cars by buying and selling young ladies?" asked Bud.

"Officer White, I'm a businessman. I have a university degree in chemical engineering and have interests in many things. I am not one of your criminals off the streets of Los Angeles. Be careful how you talk to me."

"What about pornography? Is that one of your many interests?"

Bud saw Patchett's eyes move nervously before he said calmly, "No, not one of mine. Now, officer, you are upsetting my day. You should take your concerns about 'young ladies' back to the police station. I do not hit my girls or hurt them in any way. Don't worry – they're safe with me. Goodbye, officer."

Bud drove away wondering how Patchett had figured out that he needed to protect women.

That afternoon Bud was at Lynn Bracken's house. "Yes? Oh, you're the policeman that Pierce told me about, aren't you? Why don't you come in?" invited Lynn Bracken.

"Thanks. I guess you know what the questions are going to be, too."

"You know that I'm a prostitute. I used to work for Duke Cathcart but only for a short time. I haven't seen him for years. He was soft and not very intelligent. None of his business ideas ever worked. That's all I remember about him. Would you like a drink?"

"Yeah. Whatever you're having," said Bud.

"What about this Nite Owl case? I read about it in the papers. Do you know who did it?"

29

"We think it's three blacks that we have in jail. We still want confessions, though."

"You know, Officer White, you're the first man in five years who didn't tell me that I look like Veronica Lake in less than a minute."

"You look better than Veronica Lake," said Bud with admiration.

"Well, thank you, kind sir."

"Tell me a bit more about Pierce Patchett. What are his other businesses?" asked Bud.

"He does a lot of things," said Lynn. "He plays with chemistry, he puts money into movies, he tells his girls what to do with their money. He's a good man."

"What about pornography?" asked Bud.

"Oh, no. Pierce likes to do sex, not look at it – or sell pictures of it. No, never." Lynn's answer was almost too smooth. Had she practiced it?

"I guess you think he's more good than bad. But what about his girls? Where does he find prostitutes who look like movie stars?"

"He doesn't find them," Lynn explained. "He makes them. Do you know who Dr. Terry Lux is?"

"Sure. He has a private hospital for stars with drink or drug problems. I wouldn't trust him as a doctor though. He's more bad than good," said Bud.

"Well, he's also a plastic surgeon and a good one. He keeps Pierce looking young and he operates on the girls who work for Pierce and changes them into copies of movie stars. Then they can work for Pierce until they're 30. He makes all of his girls retire when they reach that age."

"Did Lux cut you to look like Veronica Lake?"

"No, I refused. I really have brown hair, but everything else is the original me. I'll be 30 next month. I'm going to open a dress shop and have brown hair again."

"Honest?"

"Absolutely. I've saved a lot of money. A new life in one month."

Without thinking, Bud said, "Can I see you again?"

"Are you asking me for a date?"

"Yeah, a date, not a business appointment," said Bud.

◆

April 23, 1953 Ed Exley had a meeting with Dudley Smith and Captain Parker. Parker began: "Ed, we are under a lot of pressure to clear up the Nite Owl case. Lieutenant Smith and I trust that you will persuade Miss Soto to talk soon."

"Sir, I'm not sure she's ready," said Ed. "Can I try questioning Coates, Jones, and Fontaine again? If we had their confessions, Miss Soto wouldn't have to talk about what they did to her."

Smith laughed. "Ed, they have lawyers now. There is no way that they'll talk to you. It's time to stop being so gentle with Miss Soto. Give her a truth drug. Make her talk."

Captain Parker interrupted, "Ed, get her full story and solve this case. If you do, I'll make you a detective lieutenant immediately."

Ed couldn't believe his ears. "Ed," Parker continued, "you're 31 years old. Your father wasn't a lieutenant until he was 33."

"I'll do it," said Ed. "She'll talk."

Ed phoned Inez Soto. She was staying at a girlfriend's house. Her family wouldn't speak to her; they blamed her modern behavior for what had happened to her. "Miss Soto. It's Edmund Exley from the LAPD. How are you?"

"I'm terrible, and I don't want to talk to you," said Inez.

"You don't have to talk. I want to invite you to a special event. Did you know that Dream-a-Dreamland is going to open on Saturday?"

"Yes, I read about it."

"I'd like you to be my guest at the event. It should be

interesting."

"Really? Can you really take me there? I love Moochie Mouse. I love all of Raymond Dieterling's movies. Are you sure you can get us in?" asked Inez.

"Miss Soto, my father built Dream-a-Dreamland. You can meet him and Mr. Dieterling."

"Oh, that would be wonderful! I'd love to go!"

On Saturday Inez and Ed walked arm-in-arm through the entrance of Dream-a-Dreamland. Inez loved everything she saw in this magic land. She smiled and forgot about her troubles. When the two young people were in Paul's World, they found Preston Exley and the great Raymond Dieterling. "Father, Mr. Dieterling," said Ed, "I'd like you to meet Inez Soto, a friend of mine."

"Oh, Mr. Dieterling. I love this place, and I admire your work so much," said Inez. "It's an honor to meet you."

"Well, Miss Soto, I'm very glad that you're enjoying yourself. I know about your recent trouble, and I want you to know that you can have a good job here whenever you wish. Here is my business card. Give me a call when you're ready," said Raymond Dieterling in a kind voice.

"Thank you, thank you, sir," Inez said, trying not to cry.

In the car on the way home, Inez couldn't stop talking about Dream-a-Dreamland or about her hero, Raymond Dieterling.

"Inez, I'm happy that you're so happy. Things are going better for you now, aren't they? Now you know that you can trust me," said Ed.

"Ed, I had a wonderful time, but I still won't talk about that night. I'm afraid I will never trust you. You don't hate those animals the way that I do. Officer White is the only man I trust because he's the only one who understands how I feel. Good night." Inez got out of Ed's car and hurried into her friend's house.

♦

It was the morning after Ed had taken Inez Soto to Dream-a-Dreamland. He couldn't sleep; Inez had told him that she didn't trust him. Bud White was her idea of a real man. Ed didn't know what to do to prove himself to her.

The phone rang. Ed rolled over and picked it up. "Exley here."

"Good morning, Ed. It's Bob Gibson. Listen – something might be happening in the Nite Owl case. You need to be at the District Attorney's office at 8:30. I think it could be important."

"What's it about?" Ed asked Gibson, the young Assistant District Attorney.

"Last night a lawyer phoned our office and said he had two witnesses who had information that would solve the Nite Owl case for us."

"Who are they?"

"They're two brothers, Pete and Baxter Englekling, ages 36 and 32. They own a print shop in San Bernardino. They both had some trouble with the police when they were young for possessing marijuana. And we have some information about their father, 'Doc' Englekling, now dead. He was a chemistry teacher and developed some special drugs for the old Los Angeles gangsters in the 1930s. Mickey Cohen used to work for him in those days. The brothers have had some troubles with drugs again lately. They want to exchange their information for a guarantee of no jail time. Get to my office at 8:30 – this might be interesting."

Ed joined Bob Gibson and Russ Millard from Vice at the District Attorney's office. They sat across the table from Peter and Baxter Englekling and their lawyer, Jake Kellerman.

"Mr. Kellerman," Bob Gibson began, "we are interested in information about the Nite Owl murders which took place on April 14 of this year. I understand that you have a report that the Engleklings have asked you to read."

"That is correct."

"Please read the report. We will ask questions when you have finished."

"We, Peter and Baxter Englekling, swear that our story is completely true," began Kellerman. "In late March of this year, Mr. Delbert 'Duke' Cathcart visited our print shop in San Bernardino. Mr. Cathcart showed us some strange pornographic photographs. Some showed people cut into pieces and the body parts had been painted with red ink. He wanted to know if we could print these photographs quickly and cheaply to make a magazine."

Kellerman took a drink of water. "Then Cathcart said he knew that our late father, 'Doc' Englekling, had known Mickey Cohen. He asked us to get money from Cohen to start his magazine business. His plan was that we would print the magazines, he would sell them, and Cohen would pay the costs until the magazine started making money. Then we would all share the profits."

Kellerman continued, "We visited Mickey Cohen in prison, but he laughed at Cathcart's idea. He was angry and said that he'd never do business with a fool like him. We think maybe Cohen ordered someone to kill Cathcart to get the pornography business for himself. We're afraid he might want to kill us for the same reason. We swear that this report is true."

Ed Exley, Gibson, and Millard left the room to discuss the Englekling's story. "What do you think, Russ?" asked Gibson.

"First, I don't accept any connection between Mickey Cohen and the Nite Owl. He hates pornography and he doesn't murder people just because they're fools. Second, my men have been examining a pornography case for two weeks, and they haven't found anything that connects the pornography to the Nite Owl or to Duke Cathcart. We're going to forget the whole case because there aren't any clues. Third, if there was a Cathcart–Englekling–Nite Owl connection, the brothers would be dead by now, too," said Millard.

"Ed, do you have anything to add?" asked Gibson.

"Just two small points. One, Susan Lefferts was from San

Bernardino. Two, if the blacks didn't do the Nite Owl, we're looking at a very complicated case."

"I think we have the killers," said Gibson. "Let's forget about the Engleklings – they were just trying to avoid going to jail on the drug charge. We need confessions – and we need Inez Soto to talk. Gentlemen, let's get back to our real work."

Chapter 5 Vincennes' Connections

Jack Vincennes was glad to be away from the Nite Owl case. There were too many "ifs" and "buts." Inez Soto, the Mexican girl that Sugar Ray, Tyrone, and Leroy had kidnapped and left with Sylvester Fitch, was too upset to tell the police anything. There were still no guns and no car, and now the van driver wasn't sure if he had seen a purple Mercury or not. Ed Exley suggested that someone had put a purple car there to make the three blacks look guilty, but Dudley Smith said that was a crazy idea. Did the three blacks have enough time to commit both crimes in one night? Jack saw lots of possibilities, but he wanted to forget about the Nite Owl and get back to his pornography.

Bobby Inge, formerly of Charleville Street, was still Jack's only clue to the porn magazines. Bobby was gone, but Jack didn't think a lot of people knew that. He went to Bobby's old apartment and found a message under the front door: *I'll deliver your regular package tonight. 10 p.m. Whatever You Desire! L.H.*

At 10 p.m. Jack was watching Bobby's front door. A tall, handsome 30-year-old knocked on Bobby's door and waited. Eventually he gave up and went back to his car. Jack followed him to a house in the Hollywood Hills district. When the man was inside, Jack walked up to the door and rang the bell. "Yeah? Who is it?" the man inside shouted.

"I'm a friend of Bobby Inge's," answered Jack. "He sent me to pick up his package. He had to go out of town on business." The man opened the door and Jack pushed inside with his gun.

"What are you doing? Who are you?"

"What a surprise!" said Jack. "Those were the two questions I wanted to ask you. Start talking."

"Who's going to make me?" demanded the younger man.

"Me and the LAPD. Do you want to talk here or at the station?"

"OK, OK. My name's Lamar Hinton."

"I know you work for Fleur-de-Lis. Who runs it? How does it work? What do you sell?"

Lamar looked confused so Jack helped him. "I believe you have some interesting magazines and maybe even some drugs in this house – probably enough illegal material to put you in prison for about ten years. Give me what I want and you can find yourself a new life tomorrow morning."

"Pierce Patchett runs Fleur-de-Lis. He's a respectable businessman. I'm just a delivery boy."

"Patchett's address and phone number?"

"I don't know. Somewhere in Brentwood. I get paid by mail," said Lamar.

"More on Patchett."

"He sells everything: pornography, drugs, alcohol, sex equipment. He also provides prostitutes that look like famous movie stars. I've heard he's got a partner, but I don't know who he is. That's all I know."

"OK, Lamar. Get out of town tonight and don't take anything with you."

Jack went back to the police station and looked for information on Pierce Patchett. *Date of birth: 6/30/02. Businessman, chemical engineer. No criminal record. Address: 1184 Gretna Street, Brentwood.* Jack drove up to Brentwood to have a look. An enormous Spanish-style house with a lighted swimming pool and tropical gardens. Jack walked quietly along the edge of the garden and watched without being seen. Five big, expensive cars were parked inside the gates. Lots of servants around. And then the women: one almost Rita

Hayworth,★ another almost Ava Gardner.★ Amazing. Then he saw Veronica Lake★ walk through the door and into the garden. Jack – and every man at the party – couldn't take his eyes off her. Finally Jack left and went back to Lamar Hinton's apartment.

Lamar was gone. Jack looked at all the Fleur-de-Lis stuff on the shelves and realized that even after 15 years with the police, he could still be disgusted. The phone rang. Jack tried to sound like Lamar, "Yeah?"

"Lamar, tell Pierce I need to . . . Lamar? Is that you?"

SID HUDGENS!

"Uh, yeah. Who's this?" said Jack, trying to be Lamar.

The caller was gone, but Jack knew who it was. SID KNEW PATCHETT. SID KNEW LAMAR. SID KNEW THE FLEUR-DE-LIS BUSINESS.

Jack turned out the lights and ran for his car. A bullet hit the front window of the building, two more hit a tree. Jack got to his car and drove around L.A. until he was sure that it was safe to go home. When he got there he saw a *Hush-Hush* card on his door. *Malibu Rendezvous* was written across the bottom.

◆

Next morning Jack Vincennes was at his desk in the Vice Department. He was trying to make sense of all the lies he'd heard in the last two weeks. Millard wanted to forget the pornography case, although he had a report from two brothers in San Bernardino which connected Cathcart to the porn – and Jack had the magazines from Bobby Inge's garbage can that made the connection seem possible. Sid Hudgens knew about the Malibu Rendezvous. Jack was feeling nervous because he hadn't heard from Sid lately. He wanted to get his secret file from Sid.

★ Rita Hayworth, Ava Gardner, Veronica Lake: famous Hollywood movie stars of the 1940s and 1950s.

Lieutenant Smith interrupted his thoughts. "Hello, lad."

"Dudley? What can I do for you?"

"First, forget the pornography case. I want you to join the search for Sugar Ray Coates' car. Second, I want you to watch Bud White for me. He's always looking for women to help, and I need him to concentrate on his real work."

"Thanks, Dudley. I need something real to concentrate on, too," said Jack.

That night Jack followed Bud White to the Victory Motel, where he was doing containment work for Dudley Smith. Bud walked out after midnight with blood on his shirt; he had persuaded several gangsters from the Chicago area that it wasn't a good idea to start any new business in Los Angeles. Bud drove away from the motel without knowing that Jack Vincennes was following him. He went directly to Lynn Bracken's house and stayed inside.

Jack was even more confused now. Bud White visiting Lynn Bracken, the Veronica Lake-type prostitute: this meant that White knew Bracken who knew Patchett who knew Hudgens. Hudgens knew about the Malibu Rendezvous. Did they all know? Did Dudley Smith know? Jack's head was spinning; he wanted to get out of this mess.

2:20 a.m. Jack drove to Sid Hudgens' house. Sid's car was there, but he didn't answer the door when Jack knocked. He tried the door and it opened easily. The house was dark and Jack noticed a strange smell. He put a handkerchief over his fingers, turned on the lights, and saw pieces of Sid Hudgens on the living room carpet, covered in blood. Arms and legs were arranged in a strange pattern that Jack recognized. Sid looked like one of the pictures in Bobby Inge's porn magazines. Was it the work of the same "artist"? Jack bit his arm so that he wouldn't scream, then his brain started working: Get Sid's files! There were plenty of files, but none on Jack, Pierce Patchett, Lynn Bracken, Lamar Hinton or the Fleur-de-Lis. Maybe Sid hadn't kept his secret files at home.

38

5:50 a.m. Jack called the police emergency number and, using a false voice, reported the murder of Sid Hudgens. Then he went home and waited to hear the official news of the same murder. The police had no clues about the murderer. Jack was the only cop who had seen Bobby Inge's magazines and could connect them with the murder and with Fleur-de-Lis. Fleur-de-Lis – Sid – Patchett – Bracken – White? Did Cathcart and the Engleklings connect any of this to the Nite Owl? Jack didn't think so, but he had an idea about who might have Sid's secret files. He thought that he had enough information to make a deal.

Jack went home and wrote down everything he knew about Lynn Bracken and Pierce Patchett. He included lots of details about prostitution, pornography, blackmail, maybe even murder. He guessed at some things, but he was certain that he could frighten Bracken and Patchett. He drove to Lynn Bracken's house after he typed his report.

"Miss Bracken, I think you're in a bit of trouble, and I'm here to help you. May I come in?"

"What's this about?" asked Lynn Bracken.

"Sid Hudgens, Pierce Patchett, Bud White. Do those names ring a bell?"

"OK, come in. How do you want to help me?" asked Lynn as she let him in.

"Miss Bracken, I have a report here about you and your boss, Mr. Patchett. It's my report and no one else has seen it. Why don't you have a look?"

Lynn read and seemed surprised at how much Jack Vincennes knew, especially what he knew about Pierce Patchett. "Pierce did not kill Sid Hudgens. We only heard about it when we saw the newspapers yesterday."

"OK – but I think that the police would be interested in everything else I've put in my report, don't you? Especially the part about Sid and Patchett being business partners. Blackmail was their business, wasn't it?"

"What do you want?" asked Lynn.

"I know that Sid Hudgens had some secret files. I'm guessing that your boss has them."

"If he had them – and I am not saying that he does – what would that mean to you?"

"I would want him to guarantee that *my* file would remain a secret. If my file is ever made public, my report on you two will go directly to the District Attorney's office."

Jack Vincennes left Lynn's house after she had phoned Pierce Patchett for his agreement.

That afternoon, Jack was happy to return to the search for Coates' Mercury, but first he made one more stop. He visited his old drug dealer. "I'm back. What have you got for me?" Jack asked. He bought his drugs and felt ready to solve all the problems in the world.

Searching garages in the black neighborhoods of Los Angeles was hard, dirty work. No one cooperated and most people tried to make the job more difficult than it needed to be. Jack had been working with two policemen for about six hours when he heard someone from another team shout, "Hey! We've got it!"

In a dirty garage, the cops had found Sugar Ray Coates' purple 1950 Mercury, license number DG114. There was more: there were three shotguns on the floor between the seats. The cops were celebrating. They passed around a bottle of alcohol and shot their guns into the air. Jack took a big drink to get rid of the picture in his mind of Sid Hudgens' body.

Chapter 6   Quick Justice

Dudley Smith and Bud White were at the Pacific Dining Car again. Dudley said, "Lad, we found the car and the shotguns an hour ago. The bullets from the Nite Owl match the guns. The case is almost closed, but we want confessions."

"So, the college boy will interview the blacks again?" asked Bud.

Smith shook his head, "No, Exley's too soft. This job has your name on it. Meet me at the station at 7 a.m."

Bud was disappointed that he had to use his muscles, not his brain, but he couldn't argue. He didn't want to tell Smith everything he knew. "OK, boss. Thanks for dinner."

"You're in a hurry," commented Smith. "Do you have a date?"

"Yeah, with Veronica Lake."

Bud went back to Lynn Bracken's house, where he felt he had something very special and real. In their private world, Bud was gentle and intelligent; Lynn was beautiful and loving. Their love was honest and complete. They told each other everything. Lynn read to Bud from the diary that she had been keeping for 15 years; Bud told her everything he knew about the Nite Owl case. They trusted that their secrets were safe with each other.

Bud left Lynn's place in time to meet Dudley Smith the next morning at 7 o'clock, but there was a big surprise waiting for him. Russ Millard had decided to move the three suspects – Coates, Jones and Fontaine. All three of the men had escaped during the move, just before dawn. Every cop in Los Angeles was looking for them now.

Ed Exley got the news from Russ Millard before 6 a.m. He stopped at his father's house and borrowed his shotgun. He had an idea of where the suspects might be; Sugar Ray had mentioned a drug dealer when Ed interviewed him. The detective headed straight for Roland Navarette's apartment.

Ed was tense and afraid – like in the war, 1943. He found the apartment building, went up to number 408 and kicked the door in. He saw four men sitting at a table, eating sandwiches. No weapons in sight. Nobody moved.

"Stand up. You're coming back to prison with me," said Ed in an odd, high voice.

No one moved. "What's wrong, honey? Lost your voice?" asked Coates.

Ed aimed the shotgun and hit Coates' legs twice. The others

started screaming and trying to get out of the room. Ed quickly aimed again and killed all four of them. He walked out of the building and saw a crowd of cops waiting for him. They cheered and whistled. The case was closed; now Ed was the hero.

◆

The end of the Nite Owl case changed things at the LAPD. Ed Exley was still not a typical cop and he wasn't close to the men, but they no longer hated him and they followed his orders. He received the highest praise from the police department and from the city of Los Angeles for shooting the Nite Owl murderers, and he was made a police captain immediately.

Bud White started working on his career after the Nite Owl, too. He surprised a lot of people by taking time off work and studying for the sergeant's test. He passed with a high score and became Sergeant Wendell White of the Detective Department in January, 1958.

Jack Vincennes' career did not recover from the shock of Sid Hudgens' murder. Neither the murderer nor Sid's famous secret files were ever found. Jack continued to drink and use drugs and lost his job with the TV program *Badge of Honor* because of his embarrassing behavior. Although he was often drunk, he managed to stay in his job at the LAPD. He would need some luck to keep it until he could retire.

PART THREE

Chapter 7 New Jobs

January 1958 Captain Edmund Exley was sitting at his favorite table at the Pacific Dining Car restaurant. He was glad that Assistant District Attorney Bob Gibson was late for their meeting – Ed wanted a few minutes alone to enjoy thinking about his big day. In one hour he would be named Head of Internal Affairs. He had already had a brilliant career with the LAPD, but this step up would put him beyond his father's achievements as a policeman. And in a few more years he would compete with Dudley Smith for the top job: Chief of Detectives.

Ed hoped that Inez would be pleased for him today, too. After he had shot and killed the Nite Owl murderers, Ed had become Inez's hero for a time. They became lovers and Ed bought a house for her close to his apartment. Inez accepted Raymond Dieterling's offer of a job at Dream-a-Dreamland, and the older man fell in love with Inez and her sad story, too. She spent a lot of time with Dieterling and Preston Exley; she was like a daughter to them.

But things weren't perfect for Ed. He had terrible dreams about the murders. Were those four men innocent of the Nite Owl crime? Everyone at the police department was so excited about solving the case that no one looked closely at what Ed had done. When he had found the suspects at Roland Navarette's apartment, they had not had weapons. They didn't threaten Ed, but he shot all four of them. The suspects were dead, so Inez didn't have to tell her story to the police. She told Ed that the three blacks had left her with Sylvester Fitch. They had had plenty of time to get to the Nite Owl and kill the six victims there.

Time passed and Ed and Inez grew apart. She knew that he would never marry her – he was an important Los Angeles police captain, and she was a Mexican from the wrong part of town; marriage to her would ruin his career. They continued to be lovers, but their hearts were somewhere else. They were held together by a past that neither of them could forget.

Bob Gibson arrived and congratulated Ed on his new job, but he looked nervous. "What's wrong, Bob?" asked Ed. "This is supposed to be a happy day."

"It is, Ed, of course it is," said Gibson.

"Well, why do you look so worried?"

"You know that I investigated your police record and your private life," explained Gibson.

"Of course, but I'm sure you didn't find anything negative," said Ed.

"Nothing negative about *you,* but we also had to investigate Inez. Ed, I hate to tell you this: she's sleeping with Bud White."

Ed became Head of Internal Affairs that afternoon, but he didn't remember anything about the ceremony. Captain Parker made a speech, and somehow Ed himself managed to make a speech. Then he drove to Inez's house. He sat in the dark and waited for her.

"Don't turn on the lights," warned Ed. "I don't want to see your face. How long have you been sleeping with him?"

"Who told you?" asked Inez. She knew exactly who Ed was talking about.

"How long?" Ed demanded.

"For about four years. Whenever we each needed a friend."

"Wasn't I enough for you?"

"You frightened me. You wanted to prove that you were a man. With Bud, I could just be a girl seeing a boyfriend – not a police case."

"I did everything for you, Inez, and you lied to me. What other lies have you told me?"

"You don't want to know," said Inez sadly.

"Lies don't frighten me. Tell me. Now!" shouted Ed.

"Here's the only lie that's important, and it's all for you. I haven't even told Bud. The black men who hurt me couldn't have been at the Nite Owl because they were with me all night. They never left my sight. So, do you know what the big lie is? It's you – you and your absolute justice."

Ed ran out of the house with his hands over his ears. It was dark and cold outside and Ed was alone with his ghosts.

♦

Bud White had a feeling of satisfaction when he looked at his new badge: "Sergeant" where "Policeman" used to be. He was cleaning out his old desk and moving over to the Detective Department. His files and papers made him think about the last five years. He had continued to see Lynn Bracken – she was the first and only woman who he could be both friends and lovers with. She owned a dress shop now and had lovely brown hair; they were a couple but they didn't spend 24 hours a day with each other. Bud also saw Inez Soto occasionally. He didn't understand how that had happened, but she needed him and he tried to help her forget about the past. He cared about her because they had both lost so much of their youth, and she had suffered even more than he had.

After the Nite Owl case was "solved," Bud changed his style of working. He hated jobs for Dudley Smith: meeting possible gangsters at the airport and bus stations, taking them to the Victory Motel, beating them up and driving them out of town – all before they had even committed a crime. Lieutenant Smith called it *containment*; Bud called it coward's work. He avoided it whenever he could. He wasn't called the hardest cop in Los Angeles anymore, but he had been working harder than ever over the last five years.

Bud had taken several college courses in criminal psychology and police practices and had learned to use his head instead of his muscles all the time. His studies had led to his new badge and helped him with his private files on the Nite Owl case. He unlocked his drawer and went through those files – he would take them with him to the Detective Department.

The biggest file held all of his notes on the Nite Owl case. Duke Cathcart had been killed at the Nite Owl. Cathcart's prostitutes had told Bud about Duke's big plans to make and sell pornography. Cathcart's telephone book connected Cathcart to San Bernardino and maybe to Susan Lefferts. The Englekling brothers' story proved that Cathcart had been trying to make a deal. This connected Cathcart to Mickey Cohen. The Englekling brothers thought Cohen might have ordered the murders. Had Cohen intended to take over the pornography business? In 1954 the Engleklings sold their print shop and left San Bernardino. No known address. The suspects Coates, Jones, and Fontaine escaped and were shot down about two weeks after the murders. The pornography case was forgotten by the LAPD.

Problems with the Nite Owl clues: If the case was connected to the pornography, then the three blacks were innocent. If they were innocent, why was there a purple Mercury outside the Nite Owl on April 14? Why was Coates' Mercury hidden and then found with shotguns inside it?

Bud packed up his files and said goodbye to his old desk. As he walked to the elevator, Ed Exley walked past, staring at him.

Bud thought: he knows about Inez and me.

◆

January 3, 1958 Jack Vincennes was watching Hank's Ranch Market. Someone had phoned the police department with information that the place was going to be robbed that afternoon. Jack sat in his car, yawned and stretched, and then ate his lunch: potato chips and cheap wine. His stomach burned. He looked up and saw two white men go into the market; they matched the police description of the robbers. Jack heard gunshots. He raced across the street and into Hank's to find an empty cash drawer and two dead bodies on the floor. Jack started shooting and chased the robbers out of the back door. A big dog jumped out, and Jack shot it in the head, then he shot the two robbers in the back. As he tried to catch his breath, two cops in uniform came rushing up with their guns out. Jack put his hands up and shouted, "Police officer! Don't shoot!" He showed them his badge.

"Hey, I know you. You're Vincennes. You used to be some kind of TV star, didn't you?"

Jack punched the young cop in the nose and went looking for a place to drink.

Jack drank and went where he always went: back to 1953 and the pornography case that everyone else had forgotten. The Sid Hudgens' murder had never been solved, so Jack thought that maybe he could forget about his secret files. But he couldn't forget the pornography. He kept the magazines in a secret place and looked at them occasionally. The pictures excited and disgusted him.

♦

Commander Edmund Exley had his first meeting with the Internal Affairs Department. He finished his speech by saying, "Remember, we are the protectors of moral rules both inside and outside the LAPD." Ed paused, looked at his men: 22 sergeants, 2 lieutenants. "Our business is difficult: absolute justice at whatever price. Let's get to work."

After the men had gone, Ed read his speech again line by line. He heard "absolute justice" in Inez's voice. Two days ago he had believed in words like these, but Inez had made them a lie.

Ed walked into his office and looked at a report on Jack Vincennes. He was in big trouble: killing two robbers, attacking a police officer, and leaving the crime scene before finishing his official police duties. Ed looked at Vincennes' report on a pornography case in 1953 – no clues, case closed.

Ed thought about 1953. Nite Owl – Cathcart – Englekling brothers – pornography – Mickey Cohen – three dead suspects – case closed. Spring, 1953: Sid Hudgens was murdered – no suspects – case forgotten. Ed asked his secretary to find Jack Vincennes.

Jack sat opposite Ed Exley. "I knew I was in trouble, but I didn't think I'd have an interview with the big boss."

"You should lose your job," said Ed.

"Yeah. So why haven't I?" asked Jack. He thought Ed looked

strange – too thin, too old for his 36 years, too serious.

Ed leaned across the table. "In the spring of 1953 your business pal, Sid Hudgens, was murdered. Around the same time, Dudley Smith asked you to follow Officer Bud White and you agreed. This was during the Nite Owl case and a pornography case that you were working on for the Vice Department. Peter and Baxter Englekling came forward with a story about pornography, but you continued to say that there were no clues in your porn case. You were heard advising the District Attorney's office to forget about Sid Hudgens' murder. People remember that both the pornography case and Hudgens' death made you very nervous. Can you explain all of this for me, Officer Vincennes?" asked Ed.

Jack, eyes wide open, tried to speak, "How . . . did . . . you . . ."

"It doesn't matter how I found out. Tell me about it all."

"OK. I followed Bud White for Dudley, but I didn't find out anything important. Everybody knows that you and White hate each other – are you looking for information about him?"

"Maybe. What about White and women? Did White know Lynn Bracken in 1953?"

"I don't know. I never heard that name," Jack lied.

"Your face says something different, but I'll pretend that you're telling the truth. Was White seeing Inez Soto when you were following him?"

"Your girl? No, definitely not."

"OK. But what about the Nite Owl? Was it connected to your pornography case? Were the three blacks the Nite Owl killers?"

"It's not clear, but they hurt your woman, so what you did to them was right. Captain, why are you interested in . . ."

"That's my business," interrupted Ed. "But here's a theory: Sid Hudgens was connected to the pornography, and he had a file on you. That's why you kept some clues to yourself."

"Yeah," said Jack. "I did something really bad a long time ago, but, you know, I don't think I care who finds out anymore."

Ed stood up. "Listen, you're out of trouble for this Ranch

48

Market thing, and you can continue working until you retire at the end of this year."

"What do I have to do for all of that?" asked Jack.

"If the Nite Owl case is ever opened again, you and everything you know belong to me."

"OK, that's a deal." Jack walked away with one thought: he couldn't figure Exley out.

Chapter 8   Bud White's Case

Bud White moved to his new office, but he couldn't stop thinking about the old Nite Owl case. He arranged a meeting with the gangster Mickey Cohen when he came out of prison.

"Thank you for seeing me, Mr. Cohen," said Bud politely. "Could I ask you a few questions about some events from 1953?"

"When you show me respect like this, I am going to try to help you. But maybe you can help me, too. Who murdered some of my partners while I was in prison, and closed some of my businesses? And why won't my old boys – Johnny Stompanato, Lee Vachss and Abe Teitlebaum – work for me anymore? What's happened to Los Angeles while I was away? Hey, did you say your name was *White*? Are you Wendell – *Bud* – White?"

"That's me."

"I've heard of you. You and Dudley Smith and the Victory Motel, right? I should be nice to you so Dudley will be nice to me. So what do you want to know about 1953?"

"I heard that the Englekling Brothers from San Bernardino visited you in prison to get money for Duke Cathcart's pornography business. Did you discuss this business with anyone else?"

"Not a word. I'm not interested in pornography."

"Do you think Cathcart was involved in other criminal activity?"

"How do I know? Talk to someone who knew him! He was a

little fish, hoping to become a big fish. I didn't want any involvement with him. Goodbye, Officer White."

Who knew Cathcart? His last girlfriend was dead and Bud had already talked to the last two prostitutes who worked for him. The police report on the Nite Owl stated that Susan Lefferts was trying to get to Cathcart's table when the shooting began. He drove to San Bernardino for a chat with Susan Lefferts' mother.

Mrs. Lefferts wanted to let her daughter rest in peace, but Bud was holding her government check that he had found in her mailbox. "Give me five minutes of your time, Mrs. Lefferts, and then I'll give you your check. This is just between you and me. Nothing official," said Bud.

Mrs. Lefferts let him in. The only beautiful things in her small, ugly house were some photographs on the walls.

"Mrs. Lefferts, who took these photographs?" asked Bud.

"My Susie did. She studied photography at college, but her dream never came true. She died before she got a good job as a photographer."

"I'm sorry," said Bud, and then showed the old woman a picture of Duke Cathcart. "Do you recognize this man, Mrs. Lefferts? I think he was a friend of your daughter's."

"Yes, that was Susie's boss. They came here about a week before she died."

"Do you remember anything about that visit? What did they do? What did they talk about?"

"They were talking about a big business deal. They were both very excited about it. That man was sure they were going to make a lot of money. They had lunch with me and then they sat at the kitchen table and talked for hours and made telephone calls. It sounded very important."

Bud asked Mrs. Lefferts if he could use her telephone. He called the Detective Department. "Sergeant Wendell White, LAPD. I need a list of all calls to Los Angeles from this number from March 20 to April 12, 1953. The number is RAnchview

04617. Call me back as soon as possible."

The secretary in the Detective Department returned Bud's call in about two minutes. "Three calls, Sergeant. April 6 and 8, all to HOllywood 21118. That's a pay phone on the corner of Sunset and Las Palmas Street." Bud felt cold. The pay phone was half a mile from the Nite Owl Café. Cathcart and Lefferts were arranging a meeting for April 14. A disaster for them. He gave Mrs. Lefferts her check and left the house.

Bud had too much information now – he had to share it. He planned to let it out secretly through magazines and newspapers. He wanted to sit back and watch his enemy's most famous case slip away from Captain Exley again.

◆

L.A. Daily News, March 6, 1958

HERO? WE DOUBT IT!

Think back to the Nite Owl murder case: April 14, 1953. Raymond Coates, Leroy Fontaine, Tyrone Jones: do you remember those names? Criminals, definitely. But murderers? They were somewhere else that night at 3 a.m. – committing a different crime. What's our proof?

Back in 1953 two brothers connected the Nite Owl murders to a pornography business through Duke Cathcart, who died at the Nite Owl. The brothers owned a print shop and were willing to produce pornography for Cathcart. The LAPD ignored their story.

Recently a man in San Quentin Prison, Otis Shortell, told his story about April 14, 1953. He was with Coates, Fontaine, and Jones on that terrible night. They "sold" Inez Soto to him, and others, but they did not leave the crime scene all night. He is deeply ashamed of what he did to Miss Soto and wants to find peace in his heart by telling the whole truth.

Mrs. Hilda Lefferts, mother of Susan Lefferts, also murdered at the Nite Owl, has recently named Duke Cathcart as her daughter's boss and business partner. They visited the elder Lefferts about one week before the murders; she heard them talking about a big deal and about Susan's photographs. They made phone calls to a pay phone very close to the Nite Owl. Theory: they were at the Nite Owl to do business. Their

51

product: pornographic magazines. The LAPD has never talked to Mrs. Lefferts. Why not?

After the three suspects escaped from the Los Angeles jail, Edmund Exley went after them with his shotgun. They did not threaten him. They had no weapons. But he killed them for his own reasons. He went home to the beautiful Miss Soto, who he was in love with. He moved up the LAPD ladder to become Captain Exley at the young age of 31 – just one week after he shot and killed the four young black men.

Captain Exley is now Commander of Internal Affairs. We hope that the first case he will examine will be the one that made him a hero. Can we expect "absolute justice" from the LAPD?

The other Los Angeles newspapers kept the Nite Owl case on their front pages:

CITIZENS DEMAND JUSTICE – FIND THE REAL NITE OWL KILLERS

LAPD IS NOT ABOVE THE LAW – ASK EXLEY "WHY?"

INVESTIGATE THE NITE OWL – NOW!

EXLEY AND SOTO IN RICH BOY'S LOVE NEST

PART FOUR

Chapter 9   Return to the Nite Owl

March 1958   Ed Exley was at his desk in Internal Affairs when the telephone rang. He was glad that it was Captain Parker and not another newspaper reporter. "Ed, I don't want you to worry about the Nite Owl case," said Parker. "We're not going to open it again. Pretty soon the newspapers will get tired of it. Otis Shortell is a criminal. He's not a witness that we can depend on. Interest in the Nite Owl will end very soon."

"The problem is that I'm not sure that I want it to. I don't think the men I killed were the Nite Owl murderers."

"Ed, don't talk like that. Stay away from the Nite Owl. That's an order."

Of course Ed couldn't stay away from the case that had made him a hero and a captain. He was sitting in a coffee shop waiting for Jack Vincennes and studying his notes:

1) Was Otis Shortell telling the truth?
2) Were the Englekling brothers connected to the Nite Owl?
3) Was the purple Mercury a clue to the killers, or was it just an accident that it was outside the Nite Owl on April 14, 1953?
4) Did the real killers find Coates' Mercury and put the shotguns in it before the police found the car?
5) Did Mal Lunceford, former LAPD cop, have any connection to the killers or to Cathcart and Lefferts?

Ed had been reading Jack Vincennes' old police reports again, too. Jack had admitted that he had been following Bud White during the Nite Owl case but had lied in his report about what he had found out. He had failed to report that Bud White had been visiting a girlfriend during that period – Lynn Bracken.

Ed had a recent report on Bracken. She was a former prostitute; she now owned a dress shop with a business partner, Pierce Patchett, age 56. Ed had some interesting information on Patchett: he was a rich businessman, involved in prostitution, owned a lot of property. There had been a shooting in one of his apartment buildings during the Nite Owl case. Ed had looked into this case back in 1953. The shooting was in the apartment of Lamar Hinton. Hinton could not be found, but he had left behind several boxes of sex "toys." No suspects. Case closed.

Ed looked at the notes on Sid Hudgens. The actors and crew from *Badge of Honor* had been questioned because Sid did some *Hush-Hush* stories on several of them in the spring of 1953, but nothing had developed. The star – Miller Stanton – had been at a big party at the time of the murder. The director – Max Peltz – had been at the same party. Billy Dieterling, cameraman and son of Raymond Dieterling, had been at home with his best friend, Timmy Valburn, the actor who played Moochie Mouse. The art director, David Mertens, a sick man who had several serious illnesses, had been with his male nurse, Jerry Marsalas. No one was very upset by Sid Hudgens' death, but Ed thought that it had been important to Jack Vincennes back in 1953.

Jack finally arrived. Ed placed three used bullets on the table. "These bullets are from a shooting at Lamar Hinton's apartment in April 1953. They were found in a tree outside. They match bullets from your gun," said Ed.

"What else do you know?" asked Jack.

"Pierce Patchett owns the apartment building. Sex equipment was found in the apartment, and Pierce Patchett is Lynn Bracken's business partner. Bracken is also Bud White's girlfriend. You said you didn't know who Lynn Bracken was. Sex equipment and prostitutes – it's surprising that you didn't connect any of that to your pornography case. The last time we talked you admitted that Sid Hudgens had a file on you. My guess is that Lynn Bracken and Pierce Patchett were in business with Sid Hudgens. What do you think?"

"I think you're a smart cop," said Jack.

"Did you get Hudgens' file on you?" asked Ed.

"No, but I know that Patchett has it. He won't use it if I keep quiet about him and Bracken."

"And was Patchett selling the pornography from your case?"

"Yeah, but . . . " Jack tried to explain.

"Shut up. Do you have your report on Bracken and Patchett, and do you have the porn magazines?"

"Yeah, I'll give them to you if you keep my secrets and if I can be one of the heroes this time in the Nite Owl case."

"OK, but there will be three of us. We can't solve the case without Bud White," said Exley.

Jack Vincennes left feeling very grateful to Ed Exley. He had given Jack one more chance to be a good cop, and Jack decided that he wanted that chance more than anything. He promised himself that he would never touch alcohol or drugs again.

♦

Bud was at the Victory Motel that night, doing work that he hated: containment work for Dudley Smith. He returned to his apartment at 1:10 a.m., walked in and turned on the light. Ed Exley and Jack Vincennes were sitting in his living room.

"Hello, Sergeant White," said Ed. "Are you surprised to see us?"

"Nothing surprises me these days, Captain Exley."

"We have a big Nite Owl file and it looks like a lot of the clues came from you. We need to have all of your information," said Ed.

"And what happens if I don't cooperate?"

"I'll destroy you, your career and Lynn Bracken."

"Lynn?"

"Yes, she can help us and then we'll help her. I'm going to give her a truth drug and hear her story. I want you to be one of my assistants in this case. Is that OK with you?" asked Ed.

"I don't think I have any choice," answered Bud.

♦

Next morning Ed Exley had a meeting with Captain Parker and Dudley Smith. Ed was early and made notes: Patchett and Hudgens had probably been blackmailing Patchett's customers; Vincennes' report connected Patchett to Fleur-de-Lis and to pornography; Bud White connected Patchett to the Englekling brothers through their father – chemistry backgrounds; Cathcart was also connected to the Engleklings and to Susan Lefferts. Add it together: the Nite Owl was not a simple burglary that had gone wrong. There were dozens of serious crimes connected to it.

The other men walked in. Parker said, "The Nite Owl case is

open again. We have two weeks to solve it or it will be given to a different office for investigation. Gentlemen, do you understand?"

Smith jumped in, "We just got the wrong black men. It was probably some friends of Coates, Fontaine, and Jones, who made them look guilty. We'll go back to the black neighborhoods and find the real killers."

Ed smiled and appeared to agree with Smith. "Captain Parker, who's going to lead this case?"

"Ed, you've been in the newspapers too much lately. I want Dudley to be the leader."

"And do I have a role?" asked Ed. "I'm the best detective in the LAPD."

"Yes, I know, Ed. What kind of responsibility do you want?" Parker wanted to keep Ed, as well as Dudley, happy.

"I want to look for my own clues and work through the Internal Affairs office. I want two officers to serve as my assistants."

"I think that's fair, lad," said Smith. "Who do you want to work with you?"

"Jack Vincennes and Bud White."

Smith looked amazed. Parker managed to say, "Strange choices, Ed. But it's a strange case."

♦

Jack Vincennes watched Lynn Bracken walk toward the entrance of the LAPD. The last time he saw her was five years ago when they had made their deal: his report on Lynn and Pierce Patchett and Sid Hudgens' file on Jack would be locked safely away so no one would get hurt.

Lynn had brown hair and was about thirty-five years old, but she could still make people stop and stare. Her style combined intelligence, beauty, and sex. Jack wondered about her and Bud. Maybe she loved Bud because he was strong and honest; he didn't need to prove that he was a man.

Jack met Lynn at the door and said, "I didn't want this to happen."

"But you let it happen. Aren't you afraid of what I know about you?" asked Lynn.

Jack thought that there was something funny about Lynn Bracken's attitude. She seemed too calm for someone who was going to be questioned by Ed Exley. "The big boss is taking care of me," said Jack. "He'll protect me if he needs to."

"Well, you're lucky. I'm only doing this because Bud said he'd get hurt if I didn't cooperate. Enough small talk. Let's do it."

Jack led Lynn Bracken to the Internal Affairs office, where Captain Edmund Exley and a police doctor were waiting for them. The doctor had arranged needles and bottles of a truth drug on Exley's desk. Lynn sat down and the doctor gave her the drug that he had prepared for her.

"Miss Bracken, we are looking for information about several serious crimes that happened in the spring of 1953. If you cooperate and answer my questions honestly and completely, you will not be in trouble for your own actions during the period in question."

"Well, I can't lie, can I? Your truth drug will guarantee that you get the right answers."

The doctor checked Lynn's eyes and said that she was ready for questions.

Exley turned on the tape recorder and began, "Miss Bracken, how old are you?"

She hesitated and then said, "Thirty-four."

"And what do you do?"

"I'm a businesswoman."

"What was your job in April 1953?"

"I worked as a prostitute."

"Who did you work for?"

"Pierce Patchett."

"Do you know who Sid Hudgens was?"

"Yes, he was a magazine writer."

"Did Pierce Patchett kill Sid Hudgens?"

"No. He didn't know Sid Hudgens. Why would he kill him?"

Jack knew that she was lying. He knew that Hudgens and Patchett had been close business partners. Lynn seemed too calm to Jack. Something was wrong.

"Do you know two men named Lamar Hinton and Chester Yorkin?"

"Yes they worked for Pierce as drivers and delivery men."

"Does Pierce Patchett sell things like drugs, pornography, and sex equipment through a service known as Fleur-de-Lis?"

"I don't know."

An enormous lie. Jack looked at Lynn very carefully. He quickly wrote a note to Exley: *Pierce Patchett knows a lot about chemistry. She's lying. Check her blood. I bet that Patchett has given her a drug that will stop our truth drug from working.*

Ed read the note and passed it to the doctor. The doctor prepared a different drug and started to put a needle into Bracken's arm. She kicked him and when Ed tried to hold her down she scratched him across the cheek. Finally the doctor got the needle in and they waited for this third drug to start working.

"Miss Bracken," Ed said quietly, "you have said that Mr. Pierce Patchett is a businessman and that he puts deals together. Tell me about some of those deals, please."

Lynn looked at the ceiling. "He finances movies, puts money into property – that kind of thing. I remember that Pierce told me he had financed a few of Raymond Dieterling's early short movies. That's interesting, isn't it?"

The doctor passed another note to Ed about the drugs in Lynn Bracken's blood: *She has used a very rare drug that was developed for mental patients. Very few people would know that it would stop the truth drug from working.* Someone who knew about chemistry? Ed thought of his Nite Owl notes: Patchett and "Doc" Englekling – friends because they both knew a lot about the subject.

58

"Miss Bracken, we think you know a lot more than you're telling us. Don't pretend that you're stupid. This is about Pierce Patchett, pornography, Fleur-de-Lis, and a blackmail business with his partner, Sid Hudgens. This is about Duke Cathcart, who died at the Nite Owl, and his connection to Mr. Patchett's pornography business. This is about the Englekling brothers. This is also about Bud White because he has known this information for a long time but has not told his bosses at the LAPD."

"Bud can take care of himself. He said you were a smart cop."

"You don't even feel the truth drug, do you?" asked Ed.

"I feel very well, thank you."

"What else did Bud say about me?"

"He said that you were a weak, angry man who was competing with his own father."

Ed took a deep breath: "Miss Bracken, your friend Patchett is connected with every part of our case. I know much more than you think. You and Patchett can't win. I will hide any damaging information you have on Jack Vincennes; you've lost your insurance. I've got 12 days to solve the Nite Owl case and keep my career out of the toilet. You're going to help me do that."

Lynn turned on the tape recorder. "This is one of Pierce Patchett's prostitutes, for the official report. I am not afraid of Captain Edmund Exley, and I've never loved Sergeant Wendell White more than I do now. I used to be jealous because he slept with Inez Soto, but now I respect the poor girl's good sense to love Bud, a real man."

Ed took the tape out of the machine. "I'll question you again, Miss Bracken, and next time I won't be so nice. Go home." He walked outside and destroyed the tape.

Chapter 10   Painful Truths

In his office, Ed found a thick package from Jack Vincennes. It contained the magazines that Jack had kept from the pornography case in 1953. In the top magazines, he looked at pretty young people – some naked and some in wonderful clothes. High-class photography. High quality stuff. Then Ed got to the magazines at the bottom of the pile and found the pictures that shocked him. He saw the "bodies," in pieces, and then decorated with red ink that looked like blood. The style of the bodies in the magazines matched the style in which someone had cut up Sid Hudgens' body. Whoever had arranged the bodies in the magazine had killed Sid Hudgens!

AND ED KNEW MORE!

He ran down the hall to the records department and found the file on "Atherton, Loren, 1934." Pages of information and then the photos: arms, legs, heads of children laid out on white paper with designs in blood. They were exactly the same as the pornographic photographs and the same as Sid Hudgens' cut-up body. The killer from the Atherton case was out there somewhere. He had designed the pornographic pictures, and he had killed Hudgens. Ed's father had got the wrong man for the Atherton murders.

He went to his father's house that evening.

"Edmund, come in," said the older man. "I'm surprised to see you. I thought you'd be working night and day on the Nite Owl case. You look nervous, son. What's happened?"

"Father, outside of the police department, who's seen the photos from the Atherton case?"

"Those photos were locked away at the end of the case. Neither the public nor the newspapers have ever seen them. Why? What's this about?"

"Father, I'm sorry, but I have pornographic photographs and a murder that strongly suggest that either someone is copying the Atherton pictures or that you hanged the wrong man in 1934, and the real murderer is still out there cutting up bodies."

"Edmund, I did not hang the wrong man. You got the wrong man in your great case; I did not make that mistake."

"I apologize, father. I don't want to compete with you. I want your help. Is there anything about the Atherton case that you haven't told me?"

"No, Edmund. I've told you everything. How else can I help you?"

"I want to interview Ray Dieterling," said Ed.

"Why? Because one of his child stars was killed by Atherton?"

"No, because a witness has named Pierce Patchett as a business partner of Raymond Dieterling's about thirty years ago. We think that Patchett is connected to several crimes that are connected to the Nite Owl case."

"I've never heard of Pierce Patchett, and I don't want you to upset Raymond. I'll talk to him and report back to you. Will that be OK with you? But I suggest that you forget everything else and solve the Nite Owl case again. That will save your career."

Ed shook his father's hand and said, "Absolute justice. Remember that?"

◆

Bud White was doing office work for Ed Exley when Dudley Smith walked in.

"Good morning, lad. Thank you for your excellent work at the Victory Motel in recent days. It warms my heart. I'll have more important work for you soon."

"What kind of work?" Bud asked. "What's next?"

"Well, I've been involved in containing hard crime in our wonderful city for a long time. There's money in this kind of business, and soon I and a few colleagues will be sharing some large profits. As a colleague, you'll receive a handsome share of those profits. Soon, lad, we'll control all of the criminals in L. A. – from little neighborhood gangs to the big boys like Mickey Cohen. Think of the money we'll all get. Your next job? One difficult Italian that you have done business with in the past. He needs to be controlled. I'll be asking you for help in dealing with him."

61

"What and when? I'm not sure what you're asking me to do, boss," interrupted Bud.

"You'll know soon, but our main business in the next 12 days is to destroy Edmund Exley. That's been your goal and mine for the last five years, hasn't it? He's trying to destroy Lynn."

Bud's thoughts were flying all over the place. "Did you know about Lynn and me?"

"There is little that I don't know, and nothing that I wouldn't do for you. Exley has touched the two women that you love, lad. Think of ways to hurt him badly."

"Tell me what I have to do." said Bud.

"Nothing immediately. I just need to know that you are ready for this."

"Boss, what do I get besides the pleasure of seeing Exley fail?"

"Lad, you work with me on this and you'll become special assistant to me when I become Chief of Detectives. For now, stay away from Exley. I'll contact you in a day or two."

After Dudley Smith left, Bud phoned Lynn to find out about the interview with Exley. No answer. He was surprised that she wasn't home yet.

◆

Ed had one more stop before he ended his first day back on the Nite Owl case. He had a list of questions that he wanted to ask Lynn Bracken. When she came to her door, Ed was ready: "In my office you said that Pierce Patchett and Sid Hudgens were running a blackmail business."

"I don't remember saying that."

"It's in Jack Vincennes' report, too."

"I'm sure that report is full of lies. Why haven't you shown it to Bud?"

"Because he works closely with a rival of mine in the Detective Department, and I didn't want Bud to pass information to him."

"You mean Dudley Smith. I've heard Bud talk about him. I think Bud's afraid of him, so he must be a good man."

"Dudley is brilliant, but he's also evil."

"That's enough police work for today," said Lynn. "Can I give you a drink?"

"You're right. We've both had enough. I'd love to have a drink – just one."

Lynn Bracken handed Ed a drink and said, "How is Inez handling this mess? It must be terrible for her to have to go through the Nite Owl case again."

"I don't want to talk about her. She left me. She's living at Raymond Dieterling's house now."

"What about Jack Vincennes? I haven't seen his name in the news lately."

"He's ruined his career with drink and drugs. What's in the Hudgens' file on him?"

"I won't say that there is a Hudgens' file on Jack Vincennes, but if there was it would probably have information about a murder case in 1947. It happened at a dance club called the Malibu Rendezvous. Two innocent people were killed. The official report said that drug dealers shot them. If there was a file, it might show that Jack Vincennes had been taking drugs, and he was the one who shot the innocent people."

The Malibu Rendezvous was Vincennes' big case – just like the Atherton case for his father and the Nite Owl for him. Were they all false solutions? Were all three cops failures? "Jack loves alcohol and drugs," said Ed. "He gets crazy sometimes. One day he might come after Pierce Patchett to get that file – it's very important to him. Don't think he's too weak to do it."

"Do you mean the way you think Bud White is weak?" Lynn smiled and Ed thought that he would hit her. Instead he leaned forward and kissed her. They rolled to the floor and tore off each other's clothes. It was desperate, quick sex that let them stop thinking for a few minutes.

When they were dressed, Lynn poured them each another drink, and they started talking. Ed wondered who would say "Bud White" first. Lynn said it. She had a theory about herself. While she worked for Patchett she forgot about "right" and "wrong." But then she fell in love with Bud, and he was strong and honest and good. Knowing Bud made her want to find the old, good Lynn. To do this, she needed to get Patchett out of her life completely.

Ed was surprised that Lynn was so open with him. He wanted to tell her something about himself so he talked about his family. He had been very close to his mother, and his heart had broken when she died. Since then, he had tried to win his father's love by being a better cop than his dad had been. He told her about the war, about killing the four Nite Owl suspects to please Inez, and about the Fleur-de-Lis pornography. He rushed through his last story because it was so painful for him. He was left with difficult questions: How did the cut-up bodies in the pornographic magazines connect to the Atherton case and the cut-up children in 1934? What did the clues say about Preston Exley and Raymond Dieterling? He had nothing more to say. Lynn kissed his tears.

Chapter 11 The Pierce Patchett Connection

The next day Ed was writing his notes on a large sheet of paper that covered most of one wall in his office. He was adding details from Jack Vincennes' report, but he kept hearing his father's voice: "Edmund, I want to be governor of this state, and I don't want your situation with the Nite Owl to hurt me. Don't talk to anyone about the Atherton case or about Raymond Dieterling. Come to me; I'll tell you what you need to know. Between the two of us we'll find the answers." Ed had agreed, but he'd felt like a child. And sex with Lynn Bracken had made him feel dirty.

He looked at his sheet of paper. There was a line that connected Sid Hudgens to the porn case in 1953. Another line connected Pierce Patchett to the same pornography and back to

Sid Hudgens as a partner in a blackmail business. He had to remove the line that connected the pornography to the Atherton case; for now, he'd keep that a secret. A possible line went from Pierce Patchett to Duke Cathcart. Bud White's information said that Cathcart was planning to sell the same pornographic magazines and then start making more with Susan Lefferts' and the Engleklings' help. But who had made the original magazines? The line from Cathcart to the Engleklings went back to Patchett again. Everything kept pointing back to Patchett. There were too many lines to ignore.

Ed needed to understand how close Patchett and Dieterling were. Lynn Bracken said that Patchett had financed some of Dieterling's early work. The star of *Badge of Honor*, Miller Stanton, was a Dieterling child star at the time of the Atherton case. Sid Hudgens had written about Stanton in *Hush-Hush* shortly before his murder. Ed's father had built Dream-a-Dreamland for Dieterling, but Preston Exley denied knowing Patchett.

Ed thought of a new approach. He drove to Raymond Dieterling's house at Laguna Beach and went to the back door to avoid the newspaper reporters waiting in the front yard. Inez opened the door for him. "Thanks for letting me in," said Ed.

"The newspapers have been treating you very badly. You look terrible, Ed. Sit down and talk to me," Inez said in a kind voice.

"We were never very good at chatting, were we? Do you think I've ruined my dad's chances of becoming governor?"

"No, not yet. But try not to hurt him."

"Maybe you can help me," said Ed. "Do you know the name Pierce Patchett?"

"No. Who is he?"

"He's a successful businessman who had some business deals with Raymond Dieterling in the late 1920s. I need to know the details about those deals," explained Ed.

"That sounds like police work to me," said Inez.

"It should be, but if anyone else knows about this, it could cause trouble for Father. I need to know if his name is mentioned in connection with the Patchett deals. There might be some tax trouble for him, but we can help him avoid it if we find the information first."

"How far back do I have to check?"

"Go back to 1928. I know you can look at the files."

"I'll do it if it will help Preston."

"Only to help Father?" asked Ed.

"All right, for what you've done for me and for the friends you gave me, too," said Inez.

Back in his car Ed thought about his father. He had good reasons to keep his early friendship with Ray Dieterling a secret. Preston Exley believed that policemen and rich businessmen should not be close friends. It might not be good for finding "absolute justice" in criminal cases. Maybe he had broken this rule with Dieterling and wasn't proud of it. Ed could understand this – he hoped that he could understand everything else his father had done back in the thirties.

Ed met Jack Vincennes at the Dining Car restaurant. "Jack, we've got a plan to discuss. I want to bring Patchett in to the station tomorrow."

"What's the plan?" asked Jack.

"I'm closing the Internal Affairs office so that Dudley Smith and his men can't get my information. Then I'm going to bring in everyone we *think* did business with Pierce Patchett."

"What about Bracken?"

"She tried to keep herself out of trouble by telling me about the Malibu Rendezvous. I gave her my own story – I told her that you were desperate to get your file back, and you would do anything for it. I said you were crazy on drugs and drink and no one could trust you."

"But . . . boss, are you OK about the Malibu Rendezvous?"

"I'm OK, Jack, and here's your big chance." Ed showed Jack a bag of heroin, a knife, and a gun. "You're going after Patchett. He loves heroin, so you offer him some. You say you're there to get your file and to find out who made the pornography with the cut-up bodies. You do whatever it takes to frighten him and get what we want."

"What if he won't cooperate?" asked Jack.

"Then kill him."

♦

It was raining the next night when Bud reached Lynn Bracken's house. She was standing at the door, watching the rain. Bud ran up and she opened her arms to him. He whispered in her ear, "I was worried. You didn't answer your phone last night."

"I'm OK now," said Lynn.

"What did you tell Exley?"

"Things about Pierce that you already know. I'll tell you the whole story in the morning."

Bud saw that she had been crying. "Honey, what's wrong? Was Exley rough with you?"

"Not really, but I understand why you hate him. He's the opposite of all the good things you are, and he told me things I didn't want to know."

"Like what?" asked Bud.

"That Jack Vincennes is crazy and is going to go after Pierce to get his file."

"It sounds like you and Exley got friendly."

"Right now I'm exhausted."

"What really happened between you and Exley? Tell me."

"No, honey, I'm tired." She smiled just a little and he knew.

"You slept with him."

Lynn looked away. Bud hit her – once, twice, three times. Lynn did not move. Bud stopped when he realized that Lynn was another victim of a violent man.

♦

The Department of Internal Affairs was full of people who worked for Pierce Patchett. All of the clues in the Nite Owl and pornography cases were connected to Patchett in some way. But Exley still needed to prove that Patchett was involved in criminal activities that led to the Nite Owl murders. Chester Yorkin, one of the Fleur-de-Lis delivery men, was in Room 1. Paula Brown and Lorraine Malvasi, two of Patchett's "Hollywood" prostitutes, were in Room 2. In Room 3, Dr. Terry Lux and his lawyer. Lamar Hinton and Bobby Inge could not be found. Obviously, Lynn Bracken had not reported anything to Pierce Patchett after her interview with Ed. If she had, Ed believed that the people in his interview rooms would have been impossible to find.

One of Ed's men came into his office. "I've finished with Paula Brown, the one who looks like Ava Gardner. I've got the interview on tape. I've written down the main points for you."

Ed looked through the notes:

1 Witness, Paula Brown, produced a list of male and female prostitutes who work for Patchett.
2 Witness did not recognize any of the models in the pornographic magazines.
3 Blackmail: Pierce Patchett's prostitutes were paid extra money for information on the private lives of their customers; prostitutes left doors and curtains open so that Patchett's photographers could take pictures of them with important/rich customers.
4 No information about the Nite Owl case.

Ed called in Lorraine Malvasi, the prostitute who looked like Rita Hayworth.

"Miss Malvasi, read this and tell me if you agree that the information is true."

Lorraine looked at the notes and began to cry. "I can't say this about Mr. Patchett. He's too good to me. I don't want to hurt him."

"Miss, Pierce Patchett is finished. We have a lot more information on him. You should protect yourself and talk to us."

"No, I can't," cried Miss Malvasi.

"Do you know what it's like in a women's prison – especially for someone as pretty as you? Think about it," said Ed.

"All right! All right! It's not Pierce's fault. Someone made him do it," said Lorraine.

"Someone? Who?"

"I don't know who the guy was. I can't tell you things I don't know."

"But, you're saying that someone persuaded Patchett to go into the blackmail business against the customers who used his prostitutes. Is that correct?"

"Yes," Lorraine said nervously, putting out one cigarette and lighting another.

"When, Lorraine? When did this man put pressure on Patchett?"

She counted on her fingers. "It was five years ago in May. I remember because my dad died that month. Pierce told us that he had to cooperate with this man. He said he had no choice. Lynn Bracken said that if the customers didn't pay the blackmail money, Pierce would give their photographs to *Hush-Hush* – you know, that magazine."

Ed went into Room 1 to talk to Chester Yorkin. He was a thin, nervous type with odd shiny marks on his arms – maybe Yorkin used drugs and they were old needle marks. He was staring into the mirror when Ed walked in.

"OK, Yorkin, I want to know *everything*, and I mean *everything*. First, about Fleur-de-Lis, second about pornography and third about why a smart man like Pierce Patchett would trust a drug-user like you." Yorkin continued to stare at the mirror. Ed hit him in the throat and then threw a chair across the room. "Listen, Yorkin, you are not leaving here until you talk, so start talking."

"OK, OK, you're the boss. I was used in Patchett's drug tests. He tried new drugs on me to study the effects," said Yorkin.

"The whole story. Slowly," ordered Ed. .

"Pierce had some heroin that had been stolen from a Mickey

Cohen deal years ago. A man called Buzz Meeks left some of the heroin with 'Doc' Englekling, and Doc gave it to Pierce. They were old chemistry pals. Another guy killed Meeks and got the rest of the drugs – about 18 pounds of pure heroin. That guy brought it to Pierce, and Pierce has been working with it for years. When he has a new mixture, he tries it on me. He wants to develop a special drug that's exciting and cheap to make," explained Yorkin.

"Are you afraid of Patchett?"

"Yeah. He's an evil man."

"Help me with one more thing and I'll put him away and keep you safe."

"All right. Let me help you."

"Do you remember those pornographic magazines that Fleur-de-Lis was selling about five years ago? There were pictures of cut-up bodies with red ink that looked like blood."

"Yeah, I know that whole story." Yorkin rubbed his throat and coughed. "Pierce makes his prostitutes retire when they're 30 years old. A guy that Pierce knew persuaded some of the retired prostitutes to be in those pictures. The guy made some of the magazines. Then he asked Pierce for the money to produce a whole lot more. Pierce didn't like the idea so he just bought the magazines that existed and sold them through Fleur-de-Lis."

"Keep going, Yorkin," said Ed.

"The guy who made the magazines found a new partner and sent him to have a chat with the Englekling brothers. You know, to make a deal: the brothers would produce the stuff and this new partner would sell it."

Ed thought: Duke Cathcart.

"Yorkin," said Ed. "How do you know about all of this?"

"When Pierce filled me full of a new drug, he thought I was blind and deaf. I heard a lot of things when everyone was treating me like a piece of furniture."

"So the pornography business is dead, right?" asked Ed.

"No, that guy who gave Pierce the heroin loves pornography.

He's got a lot of the magazines hidden in a big garage somewhere. Pierce said the guy was going to sell the magazines all over the USA and in South America, too. He's just waiting for the right moment."

Ed thought: money. The pornography business was a risk, but Patchett and this other man still had more than 18 pounds of heroin to develop. It would be worth a fortune.

Yorkin: "Hey, good cop. I know more, just to make sure you keep me safe. Pierce has a secret hiding place for the heroin and his money. It's at his house, but not inside the house itself."

Ed kept thinking: MONEY.

"Hey, I know the new Fleur-de-Lis address where they keep all the stuff. It's 8819 Linden Street. Hey, Exley, talk to me!" shouted Yorkin.

"Yorkin, you're safe. Go and have a nice meal on me. You've earned it," said Ed.

Ed added the new information to the big sheet of paper on his wall. Someone brought the pornography to Patchett in the first place, but Patchett wasn't interested. The man with the porn magazines found someone else to work with – probably Duke Cathcart. But Cathcart had an idea: he thought he could make the pornography alone so he went to the Engleklings for help. The reason for the Nite Owl murders: someone – maybe the guy who brought the 18 pounds of heroin to Patchett – wanted to get rid of Cathcart and take over the heroin and porn businesses; killing Sid Hudgens was another step in that direction. The connection that still frightened Ed: Loren Atherton, 1934.

Ed went to Room 3 to talk to Dr. Lux. "Dr. Lux, I'm sorry that you have had to wait, but I only have two questions for you, and I promise that the answers are for my ears only."

"OK, Captain Exley, if you can promise that."

"Of course. First, did you perform plastic surgery on young men and women for Pierce Patchett, with the purpose of making these patients look like famous movie stars?"

"Yes, I did."

"Second, what do you know about Pierce Patchett and heroin?"

Lux whispered to his lawyer and then said, "Patchett has some very bad business partners who want to control all of the heroin in Los Angeles. Patchett has been working on a mixture that he calls 'perfect heroin.' I think he's almost ready to start selling it."

♦

Jack Vincennes arranged his meeting with Pierce Patchett by phone. "Yes, I'll talk to you," said Patchett. "Come to my house at 11 tonight, and come alone."

Jack was wearing a police vest that would protect him from bullets. When Patchett answered the door, Jack threw the bag of heroin at him. "Hello, Pierce," Jack said with hate in his voice. He pulled out his knife and scratched his own neck with it. Ed had told him to act like a crazy man on drugs. Jack touched the blood and then put his finger in his mouth. Pierce Patchett did not act afraid. He was calm – like a heroin user who has plenty of heroin in his pocket.

"Patchett, I know about your tests on Yorkin, and I know that the heroin came from the Mickey Cohen deal in 1950. I know about the pornography you were selling in 1953 and about your blackmail business. Now, give me my file and some information and I'll forget everything I know."

"What information?"

"Whoever killed Sid Hudgens in 1953 also made the pornographic magazines. Give me the name and you're in the clear. The Nite Owl was about pornography and heroin – yours. Do you want to go to prison for that?"

Patchett pulled out a gun and shot Vincennes three times, but the bullets hit the vest without causing any damage. Three more shots and Vincennes was hit once in the chest, from the side. He fell into a table and came up shooting, but the gun that Exley had given him wouldn't fire. He pulled the knife out and nailed Patchett's hand to the table with it. Jack felt a needle go into his neck. Then shots from behind them. Patchett screamed, "Lee, no! No, Abe, no Stomp, no!" Vincennes rolled away from the danger and crashed through a window.

◆

Jack woke up in the hospital and saw Ed Exley standing beside his bed. Pierce Patchett was dead and his house had been burned to the ground. Firemen had found Jack at the bottom of Patchett's front yard – unconscious but alive. They took him to the hospital, and doctors found that he had a strange mixture of heroin and other drugs in his blood – maybe it was Patchett's "perfect heroin." He'd be fine when they got the drugs out of his system.

One of Ed's men came into the hospital room and handed Ed two messages:

1) Inez Soto called. No information on Raymond Dieterling's money deals.
2) The bullets taken from Patchett's body matched bullets taken from two gangsters who were killed in May, 1955. Both of the dead criminals worked for Mickey Cohen before he went to prison.

"Thanks," said Ed. "Now go back to the department and phone the people from *Badge of Honor*. Tell them to come to my office at 8 o'clock tonight for questioning. And get me the file from the Atherton case, 1934. Don't open it, just get it for me."

PART FIVE

Chapter 12 The Real Criminal?

The clock in Bud's head had stopped working. He wasn't sure if it was Wednesday or Thursday. He wasn't sure what Dudley Smith would expect him to do – something about an Italian who wasn't following Dudley's rules and ways to hurt Ed Exley.

Bud hadn't seen Lynn since the night he hit her. He didn't want to be separated from her, so he went to her house, but there was no sign of Lynn or her car. He used his key and went inside.

Bud looked around the house for clues. He wanted to find out if Exley had been back again. He was searching Lynn's bedroom like a detective – looking in her drawers, in her closet, under the bed. He found her diary under one of the pillows. He turned to the last few pages and looked at Lynn's writing. She always used a gold pen with black ink, a pen that he had bought for her.

March 26, 1958
More on EE. He just left and I could tell that he was deeply embarrassed by everything he had told me. I pity Pierce, having such a frightening enemy. EE is so smart – he's always thinking except when he's making love, then his brain stops for a few wonderful minutes. He's so intelligent that he makes my Bud appear childish and less brave than he really is.

EE does everything to win praise from his father and now he has enormous questions about his father's past. He told me about some arty pornographic magazines that Pierce was selling through Fleur-de-Lis about five years ago. They had bodies that looked like they were cut into pieces. The design of the bodies matched the way Sid Hudgens' body had been arranged and the way Loren Atherton had arranged the bodies of the children he killed in the 1930s. EE thinks this proves that his father hanged the wrong man for the child murders. He thinks Preston Exley was working with Raymond Dieterling at the same time (one of the children that Atherton killed was a Dieterling child star). EE is afraid that if he solves the Nite Owl case correctly this time everyone will find out about the Atherton case and about his father's mistake. That would ruin Preston Exley's chance of becoming Governor of California and might ruin his life.

I love my Bud, but in the same situation he would just shoot everyone who was involved and then let someone else sort out the mess – maybe that Dudley Smith that he talks about.

More on this later. I need a long walk before I do any more thinking.

Bud tore the diary into tiny pieces, and then he picked up the telephone.

"Internal Affairs. Captain Exley speaking."

"Hello, Captain. I just read Lynn's diary and got the whole

story on your old man, Atherton, and Dieterling. I've got some other business to do, and after that I'll be talking. Maybe you should watch the 10 o'clock news tonight."

"I'll make a deal with you. Just listen," said Exley in a rush.

"Never," said Bud White, and banged the phone down.

Bud was full of energy now and thought he could do anything. He remembered that Mickey Cohen had told him that Teitlebaum, Vachss, and Stompanato wouldn't work with him anymore. Bud decided to find out what those three criminals were doing these days. He drove to Abe's Noshery, a little café that Teitlebaum had opened in 1950 when Mickey Cohen went to prison.

Bud walked into the café and saw the three men sitting at the counter. It had been years since he had seen them – Abe was fatter, Johnny still looked like an Italian movie star, Lee hadn't changed.

Stompanato said, "Wendell White. How are you, officer? It's been a long time, my friend."

"A very long time, Johnny, so how are you making your money now? I used to pay you for information. Remember?" asked Bud.

"Yeah, of course, my friend. Are you looking for information now? Maybe I can help you," said Stompanato.

"Maybe you can. What are you doing these days?"

"We have legal jobs. Johnny and Lee work for me here," said Abe.

"Yeah, only legal jobs," said Stompanato. He lifted his beer bottle and Bud noticed two expensive diamond rings on his right hand.

"Don't you have any *interesting* work now that Mickey Cohen is out of prison?" asked Bud.

Stompanato polished his rings on his jacket. "No, Cohen didn't want us to work for him anymore," he lied. "We're not doing anything *interesting*. I've got things contained, so don't worry about us. What are *you* doing?"

75

"I'm working on the Nite Owl case again. But right now I need the toilet." Bud walked to the men's room and watched the three men at the counter through a crack in the door. They were talking very quickly and Abe was throwing his hands in the air. Bud knew they were guilty of something. He thought about the three-man gangs who had been shooting Mickey Cohen's business partners while he was in prison.

Suddenly Bud heard the word "containment" in his head. It was Dudley's favorite big word. Their last conversation: "containing crime," "profits for colleagues," "one difficult Italian that you have done business with in the past." "Contained" did not sound like part of Johnny Stompanato's normal vocabulary.

Bud washed his face and walked out. "You know, I've got a new idea on the Nite Owl."

Calm Johnny: "Oh, yeah?"

Calm Lee: "Some other black gang, right? I only know what I read in the papers."

"Maybe, but maybe not. I think someone put the purple Mercury at the crime scene to make us think that the blacks were the murderers. I'm looking for the person who did that," said Bud.

Johnny polished his rings. Abe and Lee looked nervous. Bud said goodbye and walked calmly to his car. He stopped at the first pay phone that he could find and called the telephone company; he gave the woman who answered his LAPD badge number.

"Listen. This is important and it's *now*. Find out what calls are made from Abe's Noshery, telephone number DUnkirk 32758 in the next 15 minutes. I'll call you back then."

Bud waited and kept thinking: Dudley Dudley Dudley Dudley Dudley. Then he called the telephone company again.

"One call, Sergeant White. To AXminster 46811, the name: Mr. Dudley L. Smith."

Bud dropped the phone. Nothing was safe – not Lynn, not his badge. Captain Dudley Liam Smith was responsible for the Nite Owl murders.

Bud went to the file room at the Department of Motor Vehicles. He felt so full of energy that he could search the files and solve the Nite Owl case at the same time. He figured that Johnny, Abe, and Lee were the gunmen at the Nite Owl. He also figured that they were the three gunmen who had been shooting Mickey Cohen's "business partners" over the last five years. Dudley was the leader – he couldn't be anything else. All his talk of a job offer, profit sharing, hurting Exley were ways to persuade Bud to join his gang. "Contain," "contained," "containment," "big profits." It was Dudley trying to control all of the criminal activity in Los Angeles. But the Nite Owl was getting in Dudley's way so he needed to put the responsibility for it on another gang of black youths.

Bud rushed through the files looking for documents for cars bought or sold in early April 1953. He figured that the Mercury at the Nite Owl had been put there by the real killers. Dudley read police reports, and he knew that some young black guys had been seen in Griffith Park in a purple Mercury, firing shotguns in the air. He had put a purple Mercury at the crime scene to lead detectives to the Griffith Park blacks. Dudley probably thought that the policemen who found the blacks would kill them immediately. Case closed. Dudley didn't know that those three blacks were busy the whole night of April 14, committing a different crime. And he had no idea that Jack Vincennes would bring the suspects to the LAPD alive. Case not closed. So Dudley Smith's men found Coates' purple Mercury and put the shotguns in it. Coates, Fontaine, and Jones were killed, but Inez Soto and Otis Shortell brought the case back to life five years later.

And now Bud White was looking for Dudley Smith's purple Mercury. He knew that Dudley wouldn't have stolen a car – too much risk of being caught. Then a new idea: Dudley and his men hadn't bought a purple car – they had bought a different colored one and painted it.

The files were a mess, but Bud kept working. He went through the information the way he had learned at college, looking at the descriptions of the buyers. He searched the files for hours, and then suddenly something caught his eye: a document for a 1950 gray Mercury, bought on April 10, 1953. *Buyer: Allen Thayer, white male, date of birth 7/23/09, brown hair, brown eyes, 5'11", 275 pounds. Address: 1804 Oxford Street, Los Angeles. Phone number: NOrmandie 32758.* The document felt hot in Bud's fingers. Stupid Abe Teitlebaum had used a false name and address but his own telephone number. Then he had gone out and bought some purple paint.

Bud kicked boxes, shouted, sang. Dudley was guilty, but would anyone believe him? None of the clues actually put Dudley at the scene of a crime. Dudley was too high up in the LAPD to fall, and nobody cared the way Bud did.

Nobody, that is, except Ed Exley.

◆

Jack Vincennes was still in the hospital, but his head was clear and he was telling Ed Exley what he could remember. "I was following your orders, acting crazy like you told me. Suddenly, Patchett pulled out a gun and shot me. That stupid gun you gave me didn't work, and Patchett stuck a needle in my neck. I heard shots and Patchett shouting, 'No, Lee. Abe, no. No, Stomp no.' That's it. Everything went black after that."

From the hall, Vincennes and Exley heard Bud White shouting, "Abe Teitlebaum, Lee Vachss, and Johnny Stompanato! They killed Patchett! They did the Nite Owl!" Ed pulled Bud into the hospital room and told him to shut up. Bud looked drunk or crazy, but he wasn't either.

Jack sat up, "Bud, was it Teitlebaum, Vachss, and Stompanato at Patchett's? Tell me."

Ed was still nervous with Bud White, but he said, "Go on, White. Show us what kind of detective you are."

Bud lit a cigarette and talked to Ed and Jack like they were his students. "OK. From the beginning: Dudley Smith has been using me for muscle jobs at the Victory Motel for years. He uses some special vocabulary: 'containment,' 'contain this,' 'contain that.' The other night he told me that he needed me to teach a certain difficult Italian to behave himself. I went to Abe Teitlebaum's café yesterday to talk to Abe and his pals because of something Mickey Cohen told me."

"And the connection became clear?" asked Jack.

"Johnny made it clear," said Bud. "They all lied about their recent conversations with Cohen. Then Johnny used the word 'contained' – not a Johnny-type word. Then when I told them I had some bright ideas on the Nite Owl case, they all got really nervous. I left and checked Abe's telephone – he called Dudley Smith's house as soon as I was out of the café."

"Are you serious?" shouted Jack in surprise.

"Go on. More information," said Ed.

Bud explained about his night at the Department of Motor Vehicles. "Abe Teitlebaum bought a 1950 gray Mercury on April 10. He gave a false name and address, but the stupid fool used his own telephone number."

Ed wanted to scream: Dudley! But he said calmly, "What else do you know?"

"One of the people killed at the Nite Owl was Mal Lunceford, a former Los Angeles cop. Dudley told me to check on him, but now I think he wanted me to do a bad job, and then everyone would forget about Lunceford. I went to the file room in 1953 and there wasn't one thing about Lunceford. At the time, I thought it was because he was such a terrible cop. Now I think someone had removed his records to hide a connection between Lunceford and someone else in Dudley's gang. I think the plan was to kill both Cathcart and Lunceford on April 14. Lunceford was at the Nite Owl every night, so the killers just had to get Cathcart there, too, and shoot both of them."

Vincennes said, "Chester Yorkin told Exley that Patchett had the 18 pounds of heroin that Buzz Meeks stole from Mickey Cohen in 1950. He said that some bad guy had given it to Patchett to develop. We know that 'the guy' has to be Dudley Smith. I remember writing up reports for Dudley back in the early fifties. His story was that the heroin from the Buzz Meeks case was never found. Was Lunceford working with Dudley on that case? That's probably when Dudley got the heroin and maybe he decided that Lunceford knew too much."

Ed joined in, "Yorkin also said that the guy who brought the heroin to Patchett really wanted to sell the pornography. He was even going to sell it in South America. I wondered about the profit on pornography, but if Dudley's selling it, I can see big possibilities."

"Dudley worked for the government in Paraguay after the war. I know that, so he has all of the contacts he needs down there," said Jack.

"That's a new piece of information for me," said Ed.

"My guess," interrupted Bud, "is that Cathcart knew that Patchett didn't want to produce pornography so he went to the Engleklings and to Susan Lefferts and tried to take over the pornography business for himself. His prostitutes said he had a new dream, and it was going to make him rich. Maybe he arranged the meeting with someone from Dudley Smith's gang. He probably suggested a public place and Dudley's guy picked the Nite Owl because then the gang could kill Cathcart and Lunceford in one night."

"Dudley got rid of Cathcart and Lunceford, but imagine his shock when the Nite Owl case wasn't solved and closed on April 15. He told me to check Cathcart and Lunceford because he didn't think I was any good at real detective work. But I checked Cathcart's apartment and his phone books led me to the Engleklings and Susan Lefferts," added Bud.

"Lots of theories, but we still don't have anything that will put Dudley in prison," said Jack as he lit a cigarette and coughed. "But one more connection: the bullets that came out of Patchett matched the bullets that were used to kill some of Mickey Cohen's partners. It sounds like Abe, Lee, and Stomp have had a lot of work over the past five years from Dudley."

"Several of Cohen's 'partners' were killed while he was in prison. He told me not long ago. Those three guys will probably kill Cohen himself before long. That will help the containment plan, won't it?" said Bud.

Jack laughed. "By getting rid of all the extra players, Dudley was getting ready to sell the 'perfect heroin' and sell the pornography. He didn't warn Patchett about Exley's interviews because he was already planning to kill *him*, too. He let Lynn Bracken come and go because she didn't know about the worst stuff and she didn't know that Dudley and Patchett were working together."

"But we still don't know who *made* the pornography or who killed Sid Hudgens," said Ed. He was still thinking. "Chester Yorkin told me that Patchett had a secret hiding place outside his house for the heroin and his money. Maybe there's something there that would prove Dudley's involvement. There are guards all around the property now, but I can have them removed soon."

"But what do we do now? Stompanato is leaving town with his new girlfriend. Dudley is going to realize soon that we know," said Bud.

"I've arranged a meeting for tonight with the *Badge of Honor* people," said Ed.

"Are you looking at the Sid Hudgens murder?" asked Jack.

"Yeah. Maybe we'll get something against Dudley that way."

"I want to interview Stanton," said Jack. "We used to be good friends when I worked for the *Badge of Honor* program." He saw the look on Ed's face and continued, "It's my case, too, Captain. Patchett almost killed me."

"You're right, Jack. You talk to Stanton. We'll pick you up later." Ed and Bud left the hospital room.

"I don't think the Hudgens murder is important," said Bud. "It's all Dudley now."

"Right now we need time," said Ed.

"Are you doing this to protect your father? I thought I worried about women a lot, but you really are worried about your old man."

"Bud, think about what it will mean if we get Dudley. Let's make a deal."

"I told you I would never make a deal with you," said Bud.

"You'll like this one. You keep quiet about my father and the Atherton case and I'll let you have Dudley."

White laughed. "I think I have him already."

"Yes, but I'll let you kill him."

Chapter 13 All in the Family

The team – Exley, White, and Vincennes – were ready and waiting that night. They were waiting for the actors and crew from the *Badge of Honor* who they hoped would help them solve two mysteries: One, who killed Sid Hudgens? Two, who made the original pornography? They hoped the information they found out tonight would ruin Dudley Smith. Bud wanted to use his muscles and get some stories out of the *Badge of Honor* actors and crew fast, but Exley made the rules: no rough stuff. Bud admired Exley's brain, but he thought that Ed was stupid if he didn't know one thing: after they got Dudley, Bud would turn his attention to the "crimes" of Preston Exley.

Ed and Bud's plan was to play good cop/bad cop with Billy Dieterling and his boyfriend, Timmy Valburn – Moochie Mouse from Raymond Dieterling's television show. Dieterling and Valburn thought that they had been called in because of Pierce Patchett's murder. As Mr. Good Cop, Ed was treating the two men like guests at a tea party. They answered his questions politely. Yes, they had bought drugs from Fleur-de-Lis. Yes, they had known

Pierce Patchett socially. Yes, they had heard that Patchett used heroin and sold pornographic magazines, but they had never bought any of them. Billy Dieterling was relaxed and confident because he knew Captain Exley would be kind to him. After all, Ed's father was hoping to become governor, and his father, Raymond Dieterling, was spending a large amount of money to help him get elected.

"Gentlemen," said Ed in a louder voice, "there's another murder that happened five years ago and it was never solved. We think it might be connected to the murder of Pierce Patchett."

"Well, I'm not surprised," said Billy. "Everyone from *Badge of Honor* is here. The last time you had us all here was when that awful man, Sid Hudgens, was killed."

Bud pulled his chair up close to Billy and said, "Why did you say 'awful'? Did *you* kill him?"

"Oh, Sergeant, really. Do I look like a murderer?" asked Billy.

"Five years ago you said you were in bed with your friend here at the time of the murder. Now you say you were in bed with Timmy again when Pierce Patchett died. Very convenient. Maybe you're both murderers," said Bud.

"Captain, I don't like the way this man is talking to me," said Billy. "He's an animal."

"Sergeant, calm down and get to the point," said Ed.

"The point is," said Bud, "that Sid Hudgens loved to write about the *Badge of Honor* people. He had a big file on all of them at the time of his death. Hudgens was murdered and five years later his business partner was murdered. These two boyfriends know a lot about Patchett's businesses. I have to think that there's a connection."

Timmy Valburn said, "Captain, will you tell this man who we are?"

Exley, in his captain's voice, said, "Sergeant, these gentlemen are not suspects. They came here at my request. They want to help us."

"Well, excuse me. I thought we were trying to solve two murders," said Bud.

Exley, acting annoyed with Bud, said, "Gentlemen, please help me here. Did either of you know Sid Hudgens personally?"

Both men shook their heads, "No."

"Oh, really!" shouted Bud. "They were Fleur-de-Lis customers. They knew Patchett and they knew about his business activities. Patchett and Hudgens were partners. They knew Hudgens. Trust me – they knew him."

"Gentlemen, ignore Sergeant White," said Ed with extra care. "Could you answer a few more questions?"

"For you, of course, Captain Exley," said Timmy Valburn.

"And, Sergeant, I'll ask the questions," said Ed. "Keep your mouth shut."

"Yes, sir. You guys tell the truth. I'll know if you're lying, and you'll pay," threatened Bud.

"That's enough, Sergeant," warned Ed. "Just a few questions. First, did you know that Patchett made money from prostitutes?"

Both men said, "Yes."

Bud said, "He had boys, too. Did you guys ever use that service?"

"Not another word, Sergeant," said Ed. "Did you also know that Patchett hired a plastic surgeon, Dr. Tony Lux, to make his prostitutes look like movie stars?"

Another "yes" from both men.

"And did you know that Patchett and Hudgens had a plan to blackmail the customers who went to the prostitutes? Hudgens died, but another partner took his place in that business with Patchett. Did you know that?"

Ed was leading up to a connection with Dudley Smith. "Answer the captain, you silly boys," shouted Bud.

Billy said, "Ed, make him stop. Really, this has gone too far."

Bud laughed. "*Ed*? Oh, I forgot, boss. Your daddy is a big pal with his daddy."

"White, shut your mouth!" Ed was serious this time. "I'm sorry, gentlemen. Could you please answer the question. Blackmail – what do you know about it?"

Bud saw the two men's knees touch. He was sure that they knew something.

"We don't pay for prostitutes – male or female. We don't know about any blackmail business," said Billy Dieterling.

"You don't know anything? One of you is a famous TV star and the other one has a famous daddy with piles of money. You two are lovers! You buy drugs, you know Pierce Patchett socially! If I had a blackmail business, I'd start with a visit to you two," said Bud.

"Gentlemen, Sergeant White has a rude way of speaking, but he has a good point. Have you ever been threatened with blackmail?" asked Ed.

Valburn started to speak, but Billy put a hand on his arm and they both stayed quiet.

"Did someone come to you because he knew something about your father, Billy?" asked Bud. No one spoke. "Think, Billy. Wee Willie Wennerholm, Loren Atherton, child murders, *your father*," whispered Bud.

Billy was shaking. He pointed at Ed. "*His* father."

Timmy Valburn started to cry. Billy put his arms around him. Exley said, "You're free to go. Go home." He looked sad rather than angry.

Billy and Timmy walked out, holding hands. Ed phoned the front desk and told two policemen to follow them when they left the building.

Bud looked out of the window and saw Billy and Timmy running toward a taxi. Two policemen were following them, but they had to wait for a bus to pass. When the bus was gone, Billy and Timmy had disappeared.

Jack Vincennes was in a different room with his old friend, Miller Stanton. They had a good time telling stories and remembering the good old days when Jack had a job with the *Badge of Honor* show. He had taught Stanton how to walk and talk like a cop. They had been great pals back then, but when Jack went crazy and had to leave the show they had lost touch with each other. Remembering the past made Stanton sad, and he was also depressed because *Badge of Honor* was coming to an end. He had been the star of the show for almost ten years. He didn't know what he would do when the show wasn't on TV anymore.

Finally Jack started talking about his concerns: Patchett/Hudgens, pornography, heroin, the Nite Owl. Stanton wasn't saying much, but he looked worried. Jack knew his old friend had something he wanted to tell him.

"Miller," said Jack, "we're old friends. Is there something you want to say?"

"I'm not sure, Jack. It's really old stuff. I'm not sure if it's important to anyone anymore."

"This mess is really old, too, pal. You knew Patchett, didn't you?"

"Yeah," said Stanton. "How did you know that?"

"You were one of Dieterling's child stars. Patchett financed some of his early movies. I thought maybe you met him then," explained Jack.

"You're right. It's a terrible story, but maybe it's only important to me," said Stanton.

"Take your time, Miller. Start from the beginning and tell me all about it."

"OK. I was the fat boy in the first Dieterling movies for children. Wee Willie Wennerholm was the pretty boy, the big star. We all went to a special actors' school at the Dieterling Company and saw Pierce Patchett around occasionally. One of our teachers always talked about him – he was really handsome back them. She was a bit in love with him."

"And?" Jack encouraged Stanton to keep talking.

"Then Wee Willie was kidnapped from the school and

murdered. The police said Loren Atherton was the killer. Jack, this is the hard part."

"So, tell it fast, Miller."

"Mr. Dieterling and Patchett came to me and told me that I had to go to the police station with an older boy. I was 14 and he was about 17. They told us what to tell the police. We talked to Preston Exley, he was the detective on the case. We told him the story that Dieterling and Patchett had given us – that we had seen Atherton at the school, looking around, staring at the children. Exley showed us some photographs and we pointed to Atherton."

"And then what happened?"

"I never saw the older boy again. Atherton was hanged. Then in 1939 Mr. Dieterling sent me to the opening of a new highway. I was a teenage star by then. Preston Exley was a builder, and he had built the new highway. I heard a conversation between Mr. Dieterling, Patchett and Terry Lux – you know him, don't you?"

"Yeah, the plastic surgeon."

"I'll never forget what they said, Jack. Patchett told Lux, 'You've changed his face, and I've got the drugs that will keep him calm.' Lux said, 'And I'll get someone to watch him 24 hours a day so he won't hurt anyone else.' Then Mr. Dieterling said, 'And I gave Preston Exley someone he believes was the real murderer. Anyway, Exley owes me too much now to try to hurt me.'"

Jack held his breath, but he heard breathing behind him. Exley and White were at the door. They had heard everything.

◆

Ed sent everyone home and stared at the big piece of paper on his wall. Preston Exley was part of the big crime picture. He had known Pierce Patchett and Raymond Dieterling since the 1930s. Vincennes and White knew as much as he did, and they'd probably tell Bob Gibson. He sent them home, knowing what might happen. Ed could warn his father or not warn him and the end would still be the same.

Ed turned on the TV and saw his father opening a new highway – the biggest in California. Ed put his gun in his mouth and fired as he watched his father talk about his great achievement. No bullet that time. He held the gun against his head and fired again. Again, no bullet. He threw the gun out of the window and cried.

Hours later the telephone rang. Ed woke up from a deep sleep. "Uh . . . yes?"

"Captain. It's Vincennes. White and I are at the Detective Department. A call just came in. Billy Dieterling and another male have been found dead. Murdered. At Billy's house. We're on our way there now. Captain, are you there?"

"I'm coming. I'll meet you there."

"Captain, White and I haven't told anyone about Miller Stanton's story."

"Thanks, Sergeant."

At Billy Dieterling's house, a policeman in uniform told Ed what they knew. "A neighbor heard screams and then she saw a man run out and drive away in Billy Dieterling's car. White, early forties, average height and weight."

A newspaper reporter was already at the scene, too. Ed shouted, "This area is closed. No reporters. I don't want Raymond Dieterling to know about this yet either. Find Timmy Valburn and get him here. Now, officer."

Ed walked into the house and saw the two bodies on a sofa in the living room. There was a knife in Billy's throat and two more in his chest; the top of his head had been cut off. The other body was a white male, about forty. He had knives in his cheeks and forks in his eyes. Both men were sitting in a pool of blood and there were pills floating in the blood. Nothing arty about *this* scene, thought Ed. The murderer was wild now – no more clever designs.

Ed thought about Miller Stanton's story: "changed his face," "drugs to keep him calm," "someone to watch him so he won't hurt anyone else," "someone that Preston Exley believes was the real murderer." He followed bloody footprints into the kitchen and out of the house again.

Jack Vincennes was outside. "The other man is Jerry Marsalas. He's the male nurse who looked after David Mertens, the art director for *Badge of Honor*. Mertens was always quiet and sick – he had a serious illness, I think."

"Did he have any marks on his body that showed he had had plastic surgery?" asked Ed.

"Yeah. I saw him once without his shirt on. I was amazed to see his back – he had marks all over his neck and back."

Ed and Jack walked away from the crowd of policemen. "Mertens is the right age to be the older teenager that Stanton told us about. Maybe Lux did plastic surgery on him so that Miller wouldn't recognize him again. Captain, what are you going to do? If you continue with this, your father's going to be in big trouble," said Jack.

"I don't know. I want at least one more day to see what proof we can find of Dudley Smith's guilt. Then I'll worry about my dad."

"What do you want me to do, Boss?"

"Find White and then the two of you look for Mertens. I'll give you some men from Internal Affairs to help you. I want to keep things quiet for now."

"What do we do if we find him?" asked Jack.

"Take him alive. I want to talk to him," said Ed.

"You know, Boss, I think you're as crazy as everyone else on this case."

◆

Ed called Captain Parker and he agreed to keep the murders quiet for a while. The reporters were told that there were two dead bodies, but no one knew who they were yet. The policeman returned with Timmy Valburn. "Sir, I've got Valburn. Inez Soto is with him."

"What did Valburn tell you?" asked Ed.

"Nothing. He said he'd only talk to you. They're both in my police car."

Ed went to the car. Timmy and Inez were crying, holding each other. Inez said to Ed, "I blame you for this. Why couldn't you let Raymond and your father live in peace?"

"I'm sorry, Inez, but I don't think this one is my fault."

After Timmy had seen the bodies, Ed said, "David Mertens killed Hudgens, Billy and Marsalas, plus Wee Willie and those other children. I need to know why. Timmy, look at me."

"David Mertens. He was full of evil – that's why."

"How did it happen?" asked Ed.

"Jerry Marsalas was a very bad man. He was paid a lot of money by Raymond Dieterling to take care of Mertens and give him drugs to keep him normal. Raymond also got Mertens a job on *Badge of Honor* so that Billy could watch him, too. But Marsalas was greedy and so sometimes he gave Mertens the wrong amount of his drugs. Then Marsalas could make him do anything. He made Mertens create the strange pornography that Fleur-de-Lis was selling."

"Where did Marsalas get the models for the pornography?"

"They were some of Pierce Patchett's retired prostitutes. Jerry took the photographs and David turned them into 'art.' It was David's idea to make the bodies look cut-up – and to add lots of false blood – but Jerry was sure that the pictures would sell. He took them to Patchett."

"How did he react to the pictures?"

"Pierce didn't know that there was any connection between the pornographic photographs and the old Atherton murders, and he had no idea that David Mertens killed Wee Willie. Pierce just thought that Marsalas had some interesting pornography, but he wasn't interested in that kind of business. He bought some copies of the magazine for Fleur-de-Lis, but he wouldn't go into business with Marsalas."

"What else? Try to tell me everything in order."

"Patchett told Hudgens about Marsalas and the pornography.

Hudgens was interested because of the *Badge of Honor* connection, so he took a few copies of the magazine and tried to blackmail Marsalas. He'd keep quiet about the pornography if Marsalas gave him inside information on the *Badge of Honor* people. To stop the blackmail, Marsalas took away Mertens' drugs for a few days and made him really crazy. Mertens murdered Sid Hudgens in the Atherton style, and Marsalas stole Hudgens' most important files. He didn't know, though, that Pierce Patchett had copies of all those files already because he was in the blackmailing business with Hudgens."

"Timmy, five years ago when Jack Vincennes questioned you, did you know that Mertens had made the pornography?"

"Yes, but I didn't know who David Mertens *was*. I just knew that Billy cared about him. Since he was important to Billy, I kept quiet about him," explained Timmy.

"How did you find out the whole story?"

"After we talked to you tonight, Billy said he had to know everything. We went to his father's house and Mr. Dieterling told us what I just told you."

"Was Inez there?" asked Ed.

"Yes, she heard it all and she blames you."

"Maybe she'll understand one day. But, Timmy, why has Raymond Dieterling taken care of David Mertens all of these years?"

"David is Raymond Dieterling's other son. He's Billy's half brother. David's mother was Raymond's girlfriend. No one knew about her or her baby – not Mrs. Dieterling or the public."

Ed interrupted. "What happened tonight?"

"After Raymond told Billy the whole story about Sid Hudgens, the Atherton murders and the pornography, Billy decided to rescue David from Jerry Marsalas. But David couldn't understand who was good and who was bad. I guess he went completely crazy."

The sun came through the window. Timmy started to cry again.

Chapter 14 The Nite Owl: Case Closed

Bud White went back to Mickey Cohen's house for another friendly chat.

"Mr. Wendell *Bud* White. Come in, come in. I'm bored. Tell me something entertaining."

"Mr. Cohen," said Bud, "I came to answer both of the questions you asked me. I know who murdered some of your partners while you were in prison."

"Tell me, Officer White," said Cohen.

"Johnny Stompanato, Lee Vachss, and Abe Teitlebaum. They're part of a gang, and they got the heroin that Buzz Meeks stole from you back in 1950. They've been killing your guys, and sooner or later they'll try to kill you, too. Their gang wants to run Los Angeles. They don't like having any competition around."

Cohen laughed. "It's true that my old pals have not been ready to work with me since my return, but I don't think they have the necessary brain power to manage my businesses."

"They have help in that department: Dudley Smith."

"No. Tell me you're joking. Your big boss? Prove it to me."

"We've got lots of information, Mr. Cohen. I think for now you should get out of town until we take care of these rats," said Bud.

"Good advice, Mr. Wendell *Bud* White. I thank you."

◆

When Bud got to the police department, Exley was waiting for him. "Bob Gibson left a message on my desk. Vachss and Teitlebaum are supposed to have a meeting at Abe's Noshery at 10 a.m. I think we should go and pick them up," said Ed.

"I'll get Jack Vincennes and meet you outside," said Bud.

Abe's Noshery was full of customers. Abe was at the cash desk and Lee Vachss was sitting at a table in the back. Ed reached for his gun and remembered that he had thrown it out of a window. Abe looked up when the three cops walked through the door. Ed saw him put his hand into the cash drawer. He saw Vachss reach under his table – a flash of metal.

People were eating and talking. Waitresses were serving food. Jack walked toward the cash desk. Bud looked down the café at Vachss – he saw his gun coming up. Bud pushed Ed to the floor. Abe fired and shot Jack in the head. One bullet and he was dead.

Everyone with a gun started firing. Abe was hit several times and fell to the floor. Screams, people running, Vachss firing wildly at the door. An old man went down, coughing up blood. Bud started running towards Vachss, Ed stopped him and took his extra gun from his belt. Ed fired and hit Vachss in the shoulder. He fell but stood up again and put his gun against a waitress's head. Bud White walked towards him.

"Stop, White, or I'll shoot her," shouted Vachss.

"Leave her alone, Vachss. It's not her fight. Let her go and fight with me," said Bud.

"Don't take another step, White, or I'll shoot her."

Bud couldn't stop. He had to save the woman. When he moved forward, Vachss shot the woman in the back, then he fired at Bud. He hit Bud in the leg and in the side, but Bud kept moving towards him. Vachss fired again and hit Bud in the shoulder. When Bud got close enough, Vachss dropped the body of the dead waitress and pulled out a knife. He pushed it into Bud's chest, but Bud threw himself on top of Vachss and pounded his head on the floor until he died.

Blood was pouring out of two holes in Abe Teitlebaum's chest. Ed knelt on the floor beside him. "Tell me that Dudley Smith was responsible for the Nite Owl. Tell me, Abe."

"You already know," whispered Abe.

"Who did the Nite Owl murders?"

"Me, Vachss, and Johnny Stompanato."

Police cars were pulling up outside. Shouts. Policemen running to the café.

"Abe, the Nite Owl. Why?"

Abe coughed blood. "Drugs. Pornography. Cathcart had to go. Lunceford was part of the gang that killed Buzz Meeks. He knew who got the heroin. Get them both at the same time. Frighten Patchett." Abe tried to keep talking.

"Abe. Say that Dudley was your boss. Say it. He can't hurt you now."

"Can, too. Can hurt."

"You stupid man. Tell me," shouted Ed.

Abe was dead. The place was full of police. Several ambulances pulled up for Jack Vincennes, Bud White and the others who had been caught in the bullets. A little girl stood in the corner eating a piece of toast. Her dress had someone else's blood all over it.

Before Bud's ambulance drove away, Ed walked over and said, "Thanks for pushing me to the floor. You saved my life."

◆

Vincennes was dead and White was not expected to live. Teitlebaum and Vachss were dead. Johnny Stompanato was somewhere in Mexico. Ed had to find Mertens and find a way to ruin Dudley. He remembered that Chester Yorkin had told him about a hiding place at Pierce Patchett's house. He went there and started searching through the burned up house, garage, and yard. It was an enormous property – it would take ten men at least a week to search the place thoroughly. Ed worked his way through the house and then out to the swimming pool. Then he saw the clue he needed: there were pills floating in the water. Ed jumped in and examined the walls of the pool under the water. He found the door to Patchett's hiding place. It was already open and plastic bags were pouring out of it. Some bags were filled with pills, others with a white powder, lots with cash, and a few with papers. Ed carried bags and bags of the stuff to his car. On the last trip he had a sudden thought: he knew where David Mertens had to be.

The car heater warmed Ed as he drove to the actors' school on

Raymond Dieterling's property. Everything was quiet. It was a Sunday – no classes. It was a typical school yard except that Moochie Mouse's face was on everything. Ed walked to the corner of the yard that was closest to Billy Dieterling's house and followed a path that was marked with blood. He found David Mertens in the corner of one of the classrooms. He looked like a frightened wild animal. Ed threw the pills at him, and Mertens swallowed them as quickly as he could. He was asleep in minutes. Ed had Bud's extra gun and wanted to kill Mertens then and there, but he couldn't. He thought of the evil that this man had done, and he still couldn't kill him. Instead, he picked him up and carried him to his car.

Ed drove to Dr. Lux's hospital in Malibu. He pulled out two piles of cash and the bags of pills. He placed them on the top of the car and waited for Dr. Lux.

Lux walked up and looked inside the car. "I know that work. It's Douglas Dieterling."

"Aren't you surprised?" asked Ed.

"I haven't been surprised for many years. What do you want?"

"I want you to lock that man up and guarantee me that he will be well taken care of for the rest of his life. Here's the money to pay your bill and here are his pills."

"I accept that responsibility. Are you trying to protect your father?" asked Lux.

"I don't know."

"Not a typical Exley answer, young man," said Dr. Lux.

Ed went home and looked at what he had taken from Pierce Patchett's swimming pool. He had 21 pounds of heroin, $871,400, copies of Sid Hudgens' famous files, blackmail photographs and records of Patchett's business deals. But the name "Dudley Smith" did not appear. Nor did the names Johnny Stompanato, Abe Teitlebaum, or Lee Vachss. Ed burned the heroin but kept the files and the rest of the money.

♦

Jack Vincennes was given a hero's funeral. Bud White refused to die. He had lost over half of the blood in his body and had terrible injuries. He couldn't walk or speak. Lynn Bracken stayed at his side night and day. Ten days passed.

A large garage in San Pedro burned down. Pieces of pornographic magazines were found. The owner had been Pierce Patchett.

In his final Nite Owl report, Ed did not mention Dudley Smith. He did not say that David Mertens, murderer of Sid Hudgens, Billy Dieterling and Jerry Marsalas, was also the murderer of Wee Willie Wennerholm and five other children in 1934. Preston Exley's name did not appear in the report either.

Captain Parker told the newspapers that the Nite Owl case was finally satisfactorily closed. The gunmen were Vachss and Teitlebaum. They were trying to take over the pornography and heroin business of Pierce Patchett, who had also been murdered recently by the same two men. Ed Exley was the hero again, and again he was moved up in the LAPD. He was now an inspector.

Preston Exley announced that he was hoping to become governor of California. The newspapers said that he was a very popular choice. They said that he would win the election easily.

Exley and Bob Gibson both knew that Johnny Stompanato had been the third gunman at the Nite Owl. They had not told the newspapers this because they were still hoping to get information from him that would ruin Dudley Smith. Stompanato had returned from Mexico, but he was staying out of the Los Angeles area. Exley and Gibson were waiting for him to enter their district. When he did, they would be ready for him. Stompanato's presence in the area did not seem to worry Dudley Smith. He continued to live as if nothing had changed. Ed wanted to kill Dudley, but Bob Gibson, the only other person besides Ed and Bud who knew everything about Dudley, said it would end Ed's career. He advised Ed to wait and do things the right way. When Ed visited Bud White, though, he knew that Bud didn't want any more waiting. He wanted absolute justice now.

Chapter 15   Absolute Justice?

The TV news said that Raymond Dieterling walked through Dream-a-Dreamland every day. He had closed the park for a month when his son Billy was murdered. Ed walked up to the gate and showed the guard his badge. He found Raymond Dieterling with Inez. She walked away when she saw Ed.

"Mr. Dieterling, may I speak to you?" asked Ed.

"Please call me Ray. What took you so long?"

"Did you know that I would be coming to talk to you?"

"Yes. Your father thought that you would forget our old case. I want to tell you everything – here, in my special place," said Dieterling.

The two of them stood and looked at the mountains in Paul's World. Dieterling said, "Your father and Pierce and I were dreamers. Pierce's dreams were evil. Mine were kind and good. Your father's were bold. You should know that before you hear my story.

"I was a lucky man. I had three sons, but they were not so lucky. My first wife, Margaret, gave me Paul in 1916. While I was married to Margaret, I had a girlfriend named Faye. She had a baby in 1917: my son, Douglas. She agreed to keep the baby a secret if I gave her enough money to take care of herself and the baby. No one knew that I was Douglas's father, not even the boy himself. He thought that I was just a kind friend of his mother's.

"In 1920, Margaret died in a car accident. Two years later I married Janice, and she had Billy in 1924. Janice was a sad woman. She left me in 1930, so I was alone with Paul and Billy.

"I continued to see Faye and Douglas, but Faye became a drug user and not a very responsible mother. I was afraid that it would ruin my career if I told anyone about Douglas, so I didn't take care of the boy myself – instead, I gave his mother more money.

"At this time I was making short movies with Pierce Patchett. He brought me his ideas and paid me to produce the movies. But his ideas were evil, and I hated working with him. The movies were full of strange sex acts and odd flying animals. They could only have come from the mind of a drug user. I hated myself, too, for making these terrible films, but we made a lot of money from them. I told myself that I would use my profits from this awful garbage to make movies that were beautiful and good.

"I didn't know it at the time, but Faye had copies of these early films, and she showed them to Douglas. His poor little head was filled with terrible pictures. From a young age, he thought about nothing but sex and flying. Of course he developed into a young man with serious mental problems, and it seemed to be all my fault.

"But despite his problems and his odd imagination, I loved Douglas. He had charm, and he was handsome and intelligent. I wanted to give him some chance in life. Paul, on the other hand, was stupid and mean, although he had had every advantage in life. It always surprised me how much the two boys looked like each other, but they had very different characters.

"By the time Douglas and Paul were teenagers, I had become famous and quite rich. Douglas still lived with Faye, but he was completely wild. He started stealing, killing animals and staying away from home for days at a time. Then he met Loren Atherton. Their two strange minds seemed to fit together. They were both very sick people. They planned to build a perfect child and put wings on it. Everyone knows the details of that tragedy, but what people didn't know in 1934 was that Loren Atherton did not act alone. His partner in crime was my son, Douglas.

"Your father found Loren Atherton, and he confessed to murdering Wee Willie Wennerholm and five other children. He said that he had acted alone. He wanted to die as the 'King of Death.'

"I went to see Douglas. No one was at home, but I went into the boy's bedroom and found a trunk full of dead birds and a child's fingers packed in dry ice. I knew immediately that Loren Atherton had not acted alone.

"I talked to Douglas, who seemed very calm, and found out that he had been around my school for young actors on the day that Willie Wennerholm was kidnapped. I was responsible for making Douglas evil, and now I felt that it was my responsibility to protect him.

"I took Douglas to a famous psychologist, who promised to keep our visits secret. He said that Douglas had a rare mental disease that could be controlled with drugs. I went to Pierce Patchett. I knew that he could make the drugs for me. Then I went to Pierce's friend, Dr. Terry Lux, the plastic surgeon. Dr. Lux gave Douglas a new face; the drugs made him 'normal' and calm.

"Loren Atherton's lawyers took months to prepare for Atherton's trial. Preston Exley kept looking for witnesses to make his case against Atherton even stronger. I was still worried about Douglas so I fed drugs to him and to young Miller Stanton and taught them what to say to Preston Exley. They told him that they had seen Loren Atherton at the school alone. They hadn't told anyone until then because they were afraid that Atherton would return and kidnap them, too. Atherton did not recognize Douglas because he had a new face. Your father believed the boys' story; Atherton was hanged – case closed.

"Dr. Lux operated on Douglas again and gave him a third face, so Miller Stanton never saw the boy who had gone to Preston Exley's office with him again. I put Douglas in a private hospital, where he was given his drugs and taken care of.

"Two years passed and then your father knocked on my door again. It was the winter of 1936. Preston had news about the Atherton case. A teenager who had been at my school in 1934 said that she had seen my son Paul with Loren Atherton on the day that Willie Wennerholm was kidnapped.

"I knew that the girl had actually seen Douglas, but Paul and Douglas were almost like twins. I tried to buy your father's silence. He took my money and then tried to return it. He kept talking about 'absolute justice.' I couldn't let your father ruin my life and destroy Douglas. Instead, I asked him to keep the money and help me find a fair solution.

"Preston asked me if Paul was guilty and I said 'yes.' We agreed that we could handle the situation by ourselves. I took Paul for a camping trip in the mountains. Preston was waiting for us. He shot Paul when he was asleep, and we buried him in the deep snow. I returned from the mountains and said that Paul had been lost in a terrible accident. The world believed my story. Your father was satisfied with our solution. He left the police department and used my money to start his building business. We share our success, but we also share a tragic past." Raymond Dieterling finished his story and looked at Ed.

"Did my father really believe that Paul was guilty?" asked Ed desperately.

"Yes. Will you forgive me? In your father's name," whispered Dieterling.

"No, I can't," said Ed. "I'm going to send a report to the District Attorney's office. You'll be accused of the murder of your own son."

"I can't run away. Can you give me one week to get my business in order?"

"Yes," Ed said, and walked to his car.

♦

Ed drove directly to his father's house. He walked through the rooms and felt dirty. Beautiful furniture, thick carpets, expensive paintings – all of it had been paid for with bad money. He walked into the living room and saw his father.

"Edmund? What a pleasant surprise," said the older man.

"Father, I am reporting you for the murder of Paul Dieterling. I will return in a few days and take you to jail."

"Paul Dieterling was a killer. I punished him as a killer. I am not ashamed of my actions."

"He was innocent, and you murdered him," shouted Ed.

"Edmund, you are very upset right now. You don't know what you're talking about."

"'Absolute justice,' Father. That's what I'm talking about. It's what you taught me to believe in." Ed turned and left the house.

◆

Ed went downtown to the Dining Car restaurant: a bright place full of nice, normal human beings. Bob Gibson was waiting for him at the bar.

"Bad news on Dudley," said Gibson. "You don't want to hear this."

"It can't be any worse than what I've already heard today," said Ed.

"Well, Dudley's out of trouble. Johnny Stompanato's girlfriend's teenage daughter put a knife through his heart. He was dead before they got him to the hospital. We now have no chance of proving Dudley's involvement. All of the witnesses to his criminal behavior are now dead."

"It's not finished yet. I've got a pile of Pierce Patchett's money, and I'm going to use it to destroy Captain Dudley Smith if it's the last thing I do."

◆

Los Angeles Times, April 12, 1958

LAPD CELEBRATES: THE END OF THE NITE OWL CASE

Less than two weeks ago the famous Nite Owl case from 1953 was opened again. Police discovered a connection between the awful events of April 14, 1953 and pornography and heroin. On March 27, wealthy businessman Pierce Patchett was murdered in his own home, and two days later police officers shot and killed Abe Teitlebaum, 49, and Lee Vachss, 44, his killers. Teitlebaum and Vachss were named as the Nite Owl gunmen.

Captain Dudley Smith gave us the rest of the story: "The Nite Owl murders were committed by a gang of evil criminals who wanted to control the pornography and heroin markets in Los Angeles. They went to the Nite Owl that night to get rid of Duke Cathcart, who was trying to push his way into the L.A. pornography business. The same people murdered Pierce Patchett this year for similar reasons."

Captain Edmund Exley said that the Nite Owl case is really closed this time, although there have been stories that a third gunman died suddenly a few days ago, just before the LAPD was going to bring him in for questioning. "Not true," said Exley. "My report was complete. The Nite Owl is finished."

The Nite Owl was not only the most famous, but also the most expensive case in LAPD history. The price for solving it – in lives and in dollars – was very, very high. Was it worth it?

Los Angeles Herald-Express, April 19, 1958

DEATHS AT DREAM-A-DREAMLAND: THE WORLD ASKS "WHY?"

They were found together last week at Dream-a-Dreamland, which had been closed for one month because of the death of a great man's son. Preston Exley, 64, former policeman, successful builder, and possibly the next Governor of California; Inez Soto, 28, key witness in the Nite Owl case and advertising director at Dream-a-Dreamland. And Raymond Dieterling, 66, the brains and spirit behind America's favorite movies and amusement park.

The three bodies were lying near Paul's World, which Raymond Dieterling built in memory of his son, Paul, who was killed in a tragic accident. They did not leave a note. They took a powerful drug, fell asleep and died peacefully. Both Exley and Dieterling left fortunes. Mr. Exley's 17 million dollars will go to his son, Edmund, a Los Angeles police inspector. Dieterling left his money to several international organizations that help mentally ill children.

The world is shocked and sad. The single word *why* is on everyone's lips. Why did this tragedy happen? Miss Soto was the former girlfriend of Preston Exley's son, Edmund. She had been depressed recently because the Nite Owl case was opened again. Raymond Dieterling was in pain because of the murder of his son Billy. Preston Exley, however, had just completed a big highway and was hoping to become Governor of California. It does not seem logical that he would take his own life.

His son refuses to talk to reporters about the three deaths.

Before this tragedy, Miss Soto, Mr. Dieterling and Mr. Exley left instructions that they wanted to be buried at sea together. They were buried yesterday. There was no religious ceremony and there were no guests on the boat to watch the bodies slip into the sea.

The present Governor of California sent this message: "Very simply, Raymond Dieterling and Preston Exley represented everything that is good in our country. They were honest, hardworking, successful men who made the world a better place. May they rest in peace."

◆

Captain Parker smiled and announced the name of the new Chief of Detectives, LAPD: Edmund Exley. People clapped, reporters took photographs and Ed shook hands with Captain Parker. More hands reached out to shake Ed's hand and to congratulate him on his new job.

"Lad, you have performed well. I look forward to serving under you," said Dudley Smith.

"Thank you, Captain. I'm sure we'll have a fine time together," said Ed. Dudley smiled and walked away.

Ed looked up and saw Lynn Bracken at the door. He excused himself and went to her.

Lynn said, "I can't believe it. Instead of the Chief of Detectives with 17 million dollars, I chose a former cop who can hardly walk or talk. Oh, well, it must be love. Life's crazy, isn't it?"

Ed looked at Lynn and thought that she had grown older in the last month. She had changed from beautiful to handsome. "When are you going to Arizona?" he asked.

"Right now, before I change my mind. Bud's waiting in the car outside."

"Open your purse," ordered Ed. "Don't ask 'why' – just do it."

Lynn opened her purse, and Ed dropped a plastic bag into it. "Spend it fast – it's bad money."

"How much?" asked Lynn.

"Enough to buy Arizona. Let's go and see White." They walked out to Lynn's car. Bud's head was shaved and he was covered in bandages, but he gave Ed a funny smile.

Ed said, "I swear to you I'll get Dudley."

Bud took his hand and squeezed it. Ed said, "Thanks for your help." He touched Bud's face. "You saved me." Bud managed to laugh.

"We should go now," said Lynn.

"Did I ever have a chance with you?" asked Ed.

"Some men get the world, some men get ex-prostitutes and a trip to Arizona. You're one of the former, but I don't envy you," said Lynn, a little sadly.

Ed kissed her cheek. Bud put his hand against the glass of the car window from the inside. Ed put his hand on the outside of the glass. The car moved and Ed ran with it, hand against hand. Then they were gone.

Chief of Detectives. Gold stars on his uniform. Alone with his dead.